90 Day Leap
B. Castle

Cover Art by Steven Rice

Chapter Headings by Steven Rice

Proofread by Kayla Team

Paperback ISBN: 979-8-218-87696-8

First Edition 2025

Contents

Author's Note

Oh hey!

Firstly, thank you so much for taking a leap and jumping into my book. I hope you love it and if you don't, please don't tell me. I *will* cry.

90 Day Leap came to me during the beginning of a manic episode that honestly seemed to have no end. I sat down and wrote 30k words in three days and then didn't touch it again for months. Then I ended up on TikTok somehow and other people seemed to be a little interested (my arm was *barely* twisted, let's be real) and now here we are.

While this is a relatively low stress, fluffy, little romcom, it's not no stress. Please be mindful of the topics below:

- Dead mom club (referenced)

- Fatphobia (on page)

- Narcissistic parent

- Sexually explicit content, including but not limited to: impact play, light bondage, anal, overall just a little kinky

I didn't include it in the list above, but I do want to note that our MMC is an anxious boy. One of my favorite aspects of writing him was seeing how his running thoughts, bordering on panic attacks at times, slowed significantly the more he felt comfortable with her. On the flip side of this, our FMC is a very closed off workaholic at times, and same for her she will open up more as the book goes on.

I'll let y'all in on a little secret. They're just me and my husband. Well except for the fact that my husband can't cook to save his life and neither of us are rich and we definitely met on Tinder and not at a wedding expo... Okay, they're *kinda* me and my husband.

Anyways, please remember this is ultimately fiction. This is not a guidebook for anything. Don't reach out to me saying "B. we tried that one scene and I threw my back out!" Don't be silly geese. At least *stretch* first.

Okay, I'll shut up so you can read the book now!

Love ya,

B. <3

To my husband, for showing me what love really is

To my husband, for showing me what love really is

One

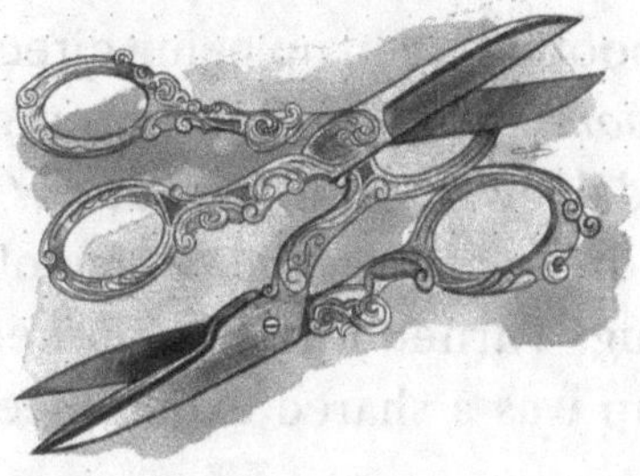

Ingrid

"**C**har, please tell me you're almost here. Desi and I are freezing, and do you have any idea how heavy this shit is?" I swore, if Charlotte wasn't my best friend, and the only one out of the three of us with a car, I could wring her neck sometimes.

"*Relax, I'm pulling in now,*" Charlotte huffed with feigned annoyance. As I heard her giggle to herself, I saw the sunshine yellow and pink floral van for her shop riding up the street. Desi and I had been standing there with all of our gear for the wedding expo for at least ten minutes. She had her jewelry cases while I was holding onto my clothing rack filled to the brim with wedding gowns. "*Okay, I'm hanging up now. Geez, did you two need to bring your entire inventory?*" She hung up the phone without waiting for a response. I could see her sly grin through the windshield as she likely continued to laugh to herself that she got the last word.

While I watched the signature *Blooming Bayne* van pull up to my shop, I took a moment to appreciate everything the three of us had created over the years. I met Charlotte Bayne and Desiree Estelle four years prior at my very first wedding expo. Our three booths ended up being directly next to each other; Char's *Blooming Bayne* floral arrangements, Desi's *Estelle Jewels* bridal jewelry, and my *Love at the Seam* bridal and bridesmaids dresses. Over the course of the day, we all ended up bonding. Turned out, all you needed to form a lifelong friendship was a shared experience with the same bridezilla.

"Char, what took you so long? It's, like, five degrees outside!" Desi yelled at Char while she bounced on her toes to keep warm. She was dressed in her tan trench coat, leggings and tennis shoes, and I could see her natural curls shake with the movement from under her pageboy cap. The sound of the little bells on her earrings jingling made me smile.

"Hey, well at least the cold is good to wake you two up," Char said as she jumped out of the van. "Would you two relax? I got coffee and the line was obnoxiously long for it being five in the morning." Somehow, even in New York in the winter, her freckles were still popping off of her face. Between that and her Irish red hair and emerald green eyes, there was no wonder she became a florist. She already appeared like the sun. Dressed in her stem green peacoat, black leggings and snow boots, she ran over to help load up the van.

Outside of my boutique, we had all of our supplies. Char kept our booth tablecloths and signage in a compartment in her van constantly since we went to expos year round, so all we needed to cram in the back were my clothing rack and Desi's jewelry cases. We'd become Tetris pros over the years, and finally had it down to an exact science.

We worked together in relative silence, just the sounds of us directing each other from time to time as we placed my dresses in the middle and then the jewelry cases past that. We learned the hard way that the lovely citizens of New York could drive fucking reckless from time to time when one year, a sharp turn to avoid collision caused multiple vases to shatter on the edge of the jewelry cases. We'd made sure to create a fabric barrier ever since.

I double checked that I still had all of our flyers and coupons in my purse as I climbed into the middle seat of the van. "Please, somebody tell me why we're even humoring this expo? It's December. Who is worried about wedding planning right now?" I asked as I grabbed my lavender latte from the drink carrier on the dash. I handed Desi her americano and did my best to get comfortable. Because I was the shortest, I always sat in the middle to make sure Desi's long legs had plenty of room. Granted, with my curves, it wasn't always the most comfy, but I didn't care. I could squish with the best of them. "I mean, we do this every year just for the winter expo to end up the biggest bust every time."

"Yeah, but it's still good for business. Plus, some of our favorite brides are from the winter expos," Desi pointed out, always the one to find a silver lining. She was good at that.

"If nothing else, free food!" Char laughed. She had a point there. If you ever wanted fancy food samples, just go to a wedding expo.

Wedding cake for breakfast didn't sound half bad, actually.

"Okay, okay, fine. You're both right. It's just so damn *cold* outside." I shivered at the lingering cold that felt bone deep. "One day, we're going to be somewhere warm, where freezing our asses off before the sun is up isn't even a concern. Just think, it's so much warmer in Italy in the winter!" Don't get me wrong, I loved New York, I did, but I could make wedding dresses anywhere and if I had the choice between New York or Italy, I would pick Italy every time.

"See, here I was thinking Greece," Desi chimed in, sipping her americano. "Just think of the jewelry there. I swear, their metal work never ceases to amaze me." Desi was a fan of all things Grecian in general. The clothes, the architecture, the mythology and of course, the jewelry. While she took inspiration from all over the world, Greek jewelry was definitely her favorite. It suited her. The gold bands with striking jewels popped on her dark complexion so well.

"I don't care where we go so long as I have room for my greenhouse," Char said as she turned onto the ferry. Our shared dream was to eventually have our own space together where all of our visions could be shared side by side. We were currently spread out a little bit in Staten Island. Not far, but not as close as we wished we could be. "I just want to grow my little flower babies next to wherever you two are."

"And you will. One day we will have all of our wishes together," I promised.

We all grew into comfortable silence once we were loaded onto the ferry to Manhattan, where the expo was taking place. With Char parked on the boat, lazily sipping her hot chocolate, I felt my phone buzz with a notification in my pocket. Desi graciously grabbed my drink from me while I pulled my phone out.

"Who in God's name is texting you this early in the morning?" Char asked from around the mouth of her to-go cup. I let out a small sigh when I saw who it was from.

"Let me guess, Senator Morgan?" Desi mused. Apparently the sigh was a tell. There was no hiding anything from those two. "What's he wanting this early?"

"He asked if I could grab dinner this week. Maybe I can just go for a casual lunch after the expo. Would you two be down to stick around for a little while once we're done?" I asked them both. I would rather not have my father bring me back home. I would also rather avoid leaving the island if I didn't have to.

"Not a problem with me, I was wanting to get some shopping done," Char said and I could already see the excitement in her eyes as she started mapping out where she wanted to go. "Desi, you in?" Desi nodded, showing the same level of excitement as Char.

Texting him back to meet at our favorite Italian place later that afternoon, I let the girls know the game plan, and did my best to ignore the looks the two of them were giving me. I could tell they wanted to say something but weren't sure if they should.

"Out with it," I sighed.

"It's just, you two confuse me. You get along with your dad, but it's like a chore for you to see him sometimes," Desi admitted. I knew it seemed like that, I really did, but it was tough when most of my life with him was spent on campaign trails, press conferences, and photo ops.

"You know I love my dad. It's not that I don't, it's just hard to feel, I don't know, like a normal person with him. Everything is just so formal, especially when we're in public. Christmas is always nice, but when we're out and about, it's hard. It's not like I have a mom around to help diffuse the tension." I didn't have much to go on about my mom outside of what my dad told me. She passed away when she gave birth to me due to complications during the delivery. I was grateful that my dad never blamed me for that, when I was sure other parents had. "He's a good dad, I know he is. I just wish it were different sometimes."

"I know, it's just weird seeing you two together. The picture perfect daughter of the beloved New York senator. Maybe when he retires, things will change with you two." Desi looked hopeful and sincere as she spoke.

"Maybe."

We spent the rest of the drive talking about the expo and letting ourselves wake up. Once we pulled in, I noticed Char straining her neck as she looked around hoping to spot somebody. "Who are you looking for?" I teased. "Maybe a cute little graphic designer?"

"Hush. I am not." Desi and I both gave her a knowing look. "Okay, so what if I am?"

"Have you even talked to him yet?" Desi mused.

"Well, no. But if he's here today then I will. I have it all planned out in my head." Char had a nervous but determined gleam in her eye.

Get it, girl, I thought to myself as I felt a surge of pride run through me.

"I'm sure you will," I said. Char had a crush on this guy, Wesley, who designed graphics for wedding stationary, signage, and wedding websites. From what we'd seen of his booth, he out-sourced for printing needs while he created the wedding websites himself. It was pretty genius, and from what I could tell, his portfolio was amazing. He'd been at the last few expos we had attended so there was a strong chance he'd be there.

Once we unloaded the van and brought all of our gear inside, we began setting up in the hotel reception hall. We regularly did combo deals to help support one another and because of that, our booths were always set up directly next to each other. With my booth in the middle, Char got all of her florals and design book arranged on my left while Desi had her cases and jewelry trees placed on my right side. After we were all good to go, we went on a hunt for the food vendors to see what sustenance we could get, namely wedding cake.

TWO

Joshua

"I can't believe you think bringing me to a wedding expo is a good way to get my mom off my back," I said to my best friend, Wes.

Wesley Wilde and I had been attached at the hip since we were in diapers. While we were on different career paths, living seemingly very different lives, I wouldn't trade our friendship for anything. Although, at that moment, I was strongly considering it as I took in the amount of *wedding* around me. Wes was a graphic designer and had been doing a lot of wedding work, so he attended expos to help build his clientele and portfolio.

"Look, you said your mom has been trying to get you set up with somebody nonstop," Wes responded. "I know this probably seems weird, but trust me when I tell you, this place is going to be crawling with single bridesmaids, cute vendors, and maybe even a widowed mother of the bride or two." He wagged his eyebrows when he said the last bit.

I just stared at him.

"This better be worth it. It's not that I don't want to meet somebody, I would just prefer *I* found them myself and not my mom. Wouldn't a bar be a better idea than this, though?" I saw his point, I did, but I didn't want a hookup bridesmaid. When my dad told me he wanted me to settle down before he handed over the reins to *Astor Investments*, I didn't disagree with him. But I was 31 years old, for crying out loud, and I had yet to find somebody that I connected with.

Wes's eyes kept darting around the room. "Just trust me, man. I swear it's not that bad." He continued searching, to the point he was almost falling over trying to look around me. We got the booth set up relatively quickly, given he didn't have a ton of props to use like some of the other vendors. We were just eating our breakfast we picked up on the way, when he seemed to have spotted what he was looking for and his eyes lit up. Looking over my shoulder, I saw that he seemed to be looking at a floral booth.

"So, are you going to tell me what you're doing right now?" I asked him with an amused laugh. He started searching our surroundings again, ignoring me completely. Once my question finally seemed to register, his face flushed ever so slightly. *Interesting.*

"The girl that runs the floral booth, *Blooming Bayne*." He nodded in the direction of the booth. "She's been at the last few expos I've been to. I'm hoping to talk to her today," he finally admitted.

"Oh? What are you needing floral arrangements for?" I teased ever so slightly. The only time I had ever seen him like that was if it was the girl herself, not whatever was around her.

"Oh, uh, you know," he stuttered. "My moms birthday is coming up, I thought maybe getting her some flowers would be nice." The blush on his face grew brighter and brighter as he muttered his way through the half assed excuse. Suddenly, the gleam went back into his eyes and I watched as he sat up straight, his eyes honing in on what I could only assume was the woman he'd been looking for. When I trailed my eyesight to follow his, I found myself holding my breath. Over by one of the wedding cake vendors, three women were all standing together, laughing and eating cake.

All three of them were beautiful, don't get me wrong, but I couldn't stop staring at the short little minx. Her laugh was the loudest, and holy shit, if it wasn't the most amazing sound I had ever heard. She was wearing a dark red sweater dress with black tights and flats. Her mid-length brunette hair fell around her shoulders in waves and looked as though it were fresh out of a beanie, a few strands sticking up in places from the small amount of static. She still had a scarf around her neck. I had to pry my eyes back to her face after I scanned every inch of her curves that her dress hugged perfectly, cursing internally as I felt my dick harden and strain against the confines of my jeans. From where we were across the room, I could just see her profile, which showcased a perfect button-like nose. She seemed to have a very small amount of makeup on, just some gloss and maybe mascara, but I could tell even from further away that she didn't need it.

As though she could feel me burning a hole in the side of her face from my stare, she turned and looked directly at me. I should have looked away. I *needed* to look away. But those *eyes*. A forest like hazel burned right back into me. I couldn't look away if I wanted to. I didn't.

I cleared my throat, careful to not look him in the eye, before asking, "Which one?"

Please don't be the minx. Please don't be the minx.

"See the redhead?" He jerked his head in the general direction of where the women were and I couldn't help but breathe a sigh of relief. I hadn't even noticed I was holding my breath while I was waiting for his answer until then.

I shifted my gaze over to the woman in question. She was cute and definitely Wes's type. I glanced over at him quickly, not ready to fully look away from the little minx who was walking toward the wedding dress booth. "Uh-huh. So, when are we going over there?"

As though he realized that I was also transfixed by one of the three ladies, his face lit up with a grin. "I told you it would be worth it." The girls had started walking over to their respective booths and I saw that they were all right next to each other, with my little minx in the center, surrounded by wedding dresses. I watched as she grabbed a sketchbook from her bag, her features relaxing into a sort of calm concentration.

Shut up. Her nose scrunches.

"What time does the expo start?" I questioned, attempting to appear nonchalant.

Out of the corner of my eye, I saw him reaching up his arm to get a better glance at his watch. "We have about half an hour."

I cleared my throat once more and turned to face my friend, making sure to shift my very obvious hard on to be a little less noticeable. Apparently I was, once again, a teenage boy who couldn't control his hormones at the sight of a pretty girl. I felt less creepy, though, as Wes needed to do the same at the sight of his flower girl. With a nod of our heads, we headed on over.

I knew I should help play wingman, but the whole reason I went with him was to try and meet a woman. So, instead of going to the floral booth on the left with Wes, I strode over to the dresses. She was still nose deep in her sketchbook, but now that I was there, I saw that all she had down was just the blank mannequin.

Interesting, I thought. *Was she trying to just seem busy after catching me staring?*

She continued staring at pad of paper as I stood directly in front of her. That just wouldn't do, so I knocked once, twice, on the booth to grab her attention.

"Good morning, sorry to bother you. My name's Joshua, or Josh, as everybody else calls me."

She finally glanced up at me, her nose still scrunched, and I was transfixed by those hazel eyes settling on me. Up close, I could see the flecks of mossy green in them more clearly. Her features relaxed as she looked her fill of me and I tried not to preen under her stare as a look of confusion dawned her face.

"Hi, Josh," she trailed off, her full lips pulling down into a pout. "I'm Ingrid. Do you need my card for your fiancé?"

Shit. Right. I'm a guy. At a wedding dress booth.

She stood and reached for her business cards when I didn't immediately answer, and I held up a hand in an attempt to stop her. "Actually, no." I scratched at the back of my neck. "I would love to get your number, though, if that's alright with you. I'm actually here helping my friend, Wes, out today. He runs the—"

"The graphic design booth, yeah!" She cut me off, looking much happier than a moment ago. "I've seen him around. His work does really well at these!" She stood on her tiptoes to look around me toward Wes's booth and I got a sinking feeling in my gut. When she realized he wasn't over there and heard her friend to our left laugh, she looked over and her smile stretched to the corners of her eyes.

Ah, the flower girl was pining for him as well.

"That's right!" I looked over at my friend and saw him gleaming at what appeared to be his source of sunlight. Looking back at my little minx, I asked, "So, tell me. When these two inevitably get married, is she going to try to do her own floral arrangements?" Out of the corner of my eye, I saw the third woman looking amused at the interactions unfolding next to her.

"Oh, she absolutely will. She's had her bouquet planned since the day she learned how to grow her own flowers from seed to vase," Ingrid laughed. She looked incredibly familiar the more I studied her face and I was sure I knew her from somewhere, I just couldn't quite place it.

"Well, on the bright side, we know who'll be designing the stationery," I joked back. "I can't help but ask, did I see you eating wedding cake for breakfast over there?" I pointed in the direction of the catering tables as I asked.

"You absolutely did. The three of us came from Staten Island this morning, and outside of coffee, there wasn't much time to get anything else," she explained with her chin raised as though she was daring me to judge her for it.

"Well, then I insist that you let me take you to a proper breakfast some time. I'll even go to Staten Island, maybe see the infamous," I started, reading the sign on the table, "*Love at the Seam* in person." The wheels were turning in her head as she considered me. She was hesitating, which was understandable. Who expected to get hit on at 7:30 in the morning?

Crap, this was technically work for her. Now I was the asshole hitting on a girl at her place of work.

As though she could see me start to panic, a playful look ran across her face.

"I'd like that. Here," she picked up one of the discarded business cards and on the back of it, I saw her writing her number.

She stepped closer and handed it to me. As our fingers grazed, I realized two things.

One, she smelled like lavender and espresso and it was intoxicating.

Two, her cheeks flushed almost to the color of her dress and her breath staggered as our hands lingered for just a moment too long.

"I'll be in touch," I looked down at the card, "Ingrid Morgan." *Ah, so that's where I recognized her from.* Senator Morgan's daughter. I could see it then. "I look forward to breakfast."

Wes seemed to have successfully placed an order for his mom, whose birthday wasn't for 6 more months, mind you, and started to walk away. As I moved to join him back to his booth, I could've sworn I heard the jeweler mutter under her breath as we passed. "What, no third guy for me?"

Three

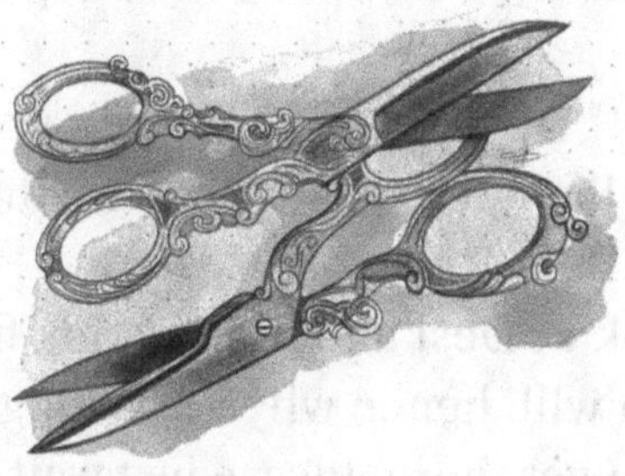

Ingrid

Shortly after Josh walked away, the expo went into full swing. I didn't allow myself a moment to look over at Wes's booth, *Heartline Designs*, and forced myself to just focus on work. The girls and I didn't have time to debrief the encounters that Char and I had, and with my lunch with my dad afterwards, I knew we wouldn't have a moment until way later in the day.

As the day was wrapping up, I checked the time and saw that it was already 1:30 P.M. Just enough time for me to close up my booth and help the girls get everything loaded into the van before I needed to leave. I was putting an A-line gown back into its garment bag when I heard Desi call out next to me.

"So, what's the plan? We clearly need to talk." I looked over at Char, and could see her nervously gnawing on her bottom lip to hide her small smile as she nodded. "Ingrid, lunch with your dad is at 2:30 right? Is it just the place around the corner?" Desi asked.

I nodded and continued working while I responded, "Yep, just trying to get everything packed up first. Once lunch is done, text me which store you two are at and I'll head over." I then pointedly looked at Char. "Don't spill a *word* until I get there!"

"Oh, come one!" Desi whined. "There's no way in hell you seriously believe I'm not going to do everything in my power to get her to spill!"

I turned to look at Desi and pointed my finger at her as I said, "I know you will, hence why I'm telling *her* to not say a damn word until I get there. Please just wait on me and then we can swap stories. Shop, spend money, have fun."

Desi finally sighed and nodded her head. "Fine, you're such a spoil sport."

After I finished packing up and started moving everything out of my booth, I chanced a glance over to where I knew he was. Sure enough, he was watching me with a knowing grin on his face, arms crossed over his chest. God, those *arms*. I swore the man looked like he ate, slept, breathed working out. Of course, he was also tall to boot. He winked at me with one of his chocolate brown eyes and turned to walk away. I watched, like a total creep, as he ran a hand through his chestnut hair as he talked to Wes.

Very tug worthy hair, I might add.

Pulling myself together, I helped the girls load up the van and said a quick goodbye. As I was walked to the restaurant, I kept thinking about the way Josh smelled like tobacco and vanilla. He didn't look like a smoker but I could see him with the occasional cigar, so I assumed it was whatever cologne he wore. He looked incredibly familiar the entire time we were talking, and while

I couldn't quite place him, I could tell he must be somebody important.

As if the universe could hear my thoughts, as I was walking by a magazine stand, I caught a glimpse of a cover that had me stopping dead in my tracks.

Right there, on the cover of a highly coveted magazine, was Joshua Astor the Third. The article was titled "*New York's Top 10 Most Eligible Bachelors*". Of course, his dad was the CEO of *Astor Investments*, the number one investment firm in the state. Without thinking twice, I bought the magazine and stuffed it into my messenger bag next to my sketchbook.

I tried to distract myself with day dreams of dresses I had yet to create as I continued on my walk toward the restaurant. *Love at the Seam* was my pride and joy. I specialized in curvy girl wedding dresses, but I offered inclusive sizing for all shapes and body types. I remembered growing up seeing the girls on TV pick out their wedding dresses, and I couldn't help but notice how the girls that looked like me never had the same amount of choices. As the girls' sizes went up, the options dwindled. I knew I didn't want to be the girl that was limited, so I dedicated my life to crafting gorgeous gowns for women like me and beyond.

I was imagining my own dream gown for the millionth time as I approached the restaurant. Walking into *Fresco dalla Vite*, I quickly scanned the tables to find my dad. I spotted him at our usual table by the window and made my way over. He looked tired, which made sense. He didn't live in the city, but instead, over in Newburgh. With the election season coming to an end, he must have been exhausted.

When he saw me walking over his eyes lit up like any normal father would after seeing his daughter for the first time in months, and I was reminded by what could be. He immediately stood to give me a hug.

"Ingrid, hey sweetheart. It's been too long." I squeezed him tight before taking the seat across from his.

"I know, I'm sorry dad. Work's been crazy with the fall wedding season and then designing the upcoming spring line," I said apologetically. I had no reason to lie to my father, work had been busy, but I hadn't made the effort to reach out to him all that much, either.

"I'm so proud of you, sweetie. I saw your dresses in that bridal magazine recently. They're gorgeous."

The waiter appeared to take our orders and we promptly placed them. As always, we requested an order of fried calamari for the appetizer, chicken piccata for myself, and carbonara for him. When we found *Fresco dalla Vite* a few years back, we both fell in love with it. It became our spot so that every time we met up we always had a place to go and our orders never changed.

"So, tell me, what have you been up to outside of work? Will you be bringing somebody home for the holidays?" I coughed in an attempt to cover up choking on a sip of water. He wanted me to settle down and spend some time to myself, but I just didn't have the time to do that. Of course, ironically, I ended up meeting a guy that day, but there was no way I could tell him that.

"Mostly just work and spending time with the girls. I was actually wanting to talk to you about the holidays to see if it would be alright if I brought them." I remained casual as I swirled my finger over the condensation on my glass, avoiding the obvious question he was really asking. "Desi's family is away overseas travelling and you know how Char's parents are." I loved Charlotte, but her family drove me fucking nuts. They had practically excommunicated her because she didn't want to do something they considered "meaningful" with her life. They would rather she went into law like they did, but no, my green thumbed friend just *had* to be a florist. Desiree's parents were a different story. They loved her, but after finally being empty nesters once her younger siblings moved out, all they did was travel. They sent us post cards and meant well, but it grew lonely for her during the holiday season.

Doing his best to hide his sigh of frustration at my avoidance, he finally said, "Of course they can come. I know how much they mean to you and you know that I love them like they're my own. I assumed they would be coming this year, anyway." I could tell he genuinely meant that. It always seemed like he felt bad for never remarrying resulting in me being an only child. He loved that I found Desi and Char, but I could tell he wished he was able to give me more.

Our waiter returned with our appetizer and drinks and we gradually started grazing. I could tell something else was bothering him, that there was something right on the tip of his tongue as he studied me.

"Ingrid, are you happy?" While I was expecting *something*, I wasn't expecting that to be the question he would end up asking me. Was I happy? I thought in the grand overarching way, yes, I was. Did I want more for my life? Goals that I aspired to? Of course, but at 27 years old, I believed they were all still very attainable.

"I just worry about you, kiddo. I see how hard you're working and again, I am so very proud of you. I would just hate for you to look back on your life later and see what you missed out on. I want you to marry the love of your life in one of the beautiful gowns you've designed, and I want to walk you down that aisle. With you getting older, and the stress of my work, I sometimes worry that I won't be able to see that day. I just want to see you get every joy you deserve in life."

I studied him as I observed the worry lines on his face and the way he seemed slightly winded from his explanation. That was one of the few times that I was able to look at him and not see my dad, Senator Morgan, but just, my dad. I took a few more bites of my calamari and a sip of my water while I worked on my response to him. Finally, I inhaled a deep breath and looked directly at him.

"I don't want you to think that I haven't settled down yet because it isn't something I desire, dad. I want all of those things that you mentioned and then some. I want to be able to design my gown, have you walk me down the aisle, and live happily ever after. I want to travel the world and have my girls by my side when I do it. I have many dreams and goals, but ending up a lonely seamstress isn't one of them, I promise." I took another sip of my water, needing a breath, before saying, "Now that my workload is starting to lighten up some, I'm planning on going out more and living a life outside of work. I can't promise that I will marry somebody tomorrow, but I'm not opposed to meeting someone."

That seemed to appease him. His eyes instantly lit up as though the idea of me simply getting myself out there more was enough to placate him. But I knew better. If I were to tell him that I had an unscheduled breakfast date with *the* Joshua Astor the Third, he would lose his mind with joy. He would already be on the phone with everybody he knew to brag about me. But I couldn't do that, not yet at least.

The rest of the lunch went on as normal. He told me about the election and his win. We talked about the holidays, the wedding expo *sans Josh*, the girls, and what weddings I had coming up. Once we finished with our meal, he got the bill and gave me a hug goodbye.

"Take care of yourself, kiddo. I love you."

"I will. Love you, too, dad."

As I left the restaurant, I checked my phone to see where the girls were. I didn't miss the fact that I had yet to receive a text from Josh. Refusing to let it worry me, I saw the girls were at *Velvet & Vice*, a newer boutique that opened up around the corner.

I made it to the shop and spotted them instantly. Desi was looking at an emerald green, crushed velvet dress while Char was admiring a pair of red satin heels. Once they saw me, they both dropped what they were doing and marched over, bags in tow from where they were previously.

"Time to hit the road! Let's go, I'm ready for the details," Desi exclaimed as she dragged Char and I all the way back to the van. Once the shopping bags were loaded into the back, we climbed in and began the drive. Char told us all about how Wes didn't ask her out but placed an order for flowers for his mom. She did her best to hide the hint of disappointment on her face, but it was quickly recovered when Desi and I reminded her that it meant she had his number and would have to see him again.

Then, it was my turn. I was telling them about mine and Josh's conversation when I felt my phone vibrate in my pocket. Grabbing it, I saw that I had a single notification from an unknown number.

Unknown Contact

So, tell me, little minx. Waffles or pancakes?

Four

Joshua

Back at the penthouse, I was on the phone with my mom. I didn't tell her about where I went earlier that day, for obvious reasons. She'd already tried setting me up with countless women, the last thing I needed her to know was that I had just been at a wedding expo filled with women. As much as I would love to think that she wouldn't try to get me to ruin an engagement with a soon to be bride, I didn't put it past her. The woman was on a mission.

I wanted nothing more than to settle down and have a woman I loved in my bed every night, but I didn't want them to be somebody my mother picked out for me.

I tuned her out while she mentioned some woman named Ashley or Bethany as I checked my text thread with Ingrid. After much deliberation, I finally crafted the perfect message to send her and the lack of response was sending me into a mild panic.

Should I maybe not have called her minx so early on? Was it too forward?

Just as I was staring at the read receipt, the bubble indicating that she was typing popped up and I shot straight up from where I was laying on my bed.

Wait, now it's gone. No response appeared. *Oh wait, she's typing again.*

Aaaand she stopped.

Come on, little minx. Waffles or pancakes. Easy question.

I placed a well timed "uh-huh, I hear you mom" when it seemed she'd caught on to the fact that I wasn't paying attention, when a response finally came through.

Minx

Do I have to choose? I love them both, but which one I want depends on my mood.

Okay, I could work with that. I needed to win her over and I thought I knew just the way to do it.

Fair point. Can you tell me if you like any fillings or toppings?

Minx

Hmm, in pancakes I prefer chocolate chips and chocolate sauce on top. For waffles, I like strawberries and whipped cream

I like those too, but I'm no longer thinking about breakfast items, I thought. *Kill me now.*

And it was officially time to end the call with my mother.

"Hey mom, yeah, I hear where you're coming from. Listen, I would really prefer to find a woman on my own. I appreciate everything you're doing, but I would love to just meet the woman of my dreams organically. I hope you can understand that." I was trying to let her down easy. There was no way any woman she found would top my little minx.

Great, now I'm just thinking about her on top.

"I understand, sweetie, I do. I just worry that's all," she said, and I could hear the guilt tripping that laced her tone.

"I appreciate it, mom. I have some work I need to get done tonight, so I need to get going. I'll talk to you later. Love you."

The moment I ended the call, I turned my attention right back to Ingrid.

> I can work with that. What're you doing tomorrow morning?

Minx

> I always close the day after expos to get any new orders organized. This being a winter expo, I actually don't have much outside of working on the spring collection. What were you thinking?

> I was thinking that it's time for you to have a proper breakfast. Be up by 9 am and I need your address.

Minx

> My address? I thought we were going out for break-fast?

> Didn't anybody tell you that I'm actually the best chef around? Address, little minx. I promise to not be an ax murderer.

Minx

Fine, but I'm trusting you, Joshua Astor the Third. There will be very angry brides for you to deal with if I don't live to release more neatly arranged white taffeta.

My address is on my card. I live above the shop. See you in the morning xx

Huh. Well, wasn't that handy. It also sounded incredibly unsafe, but I guessed as long as she was discreet about the fact that she lived upstairs, she wouldn't need to worry about the bridezillas. Also, note to self, she figured out my identity and she could never learn my middle name because she seemed like the *type*.

Government name and all? I cross my heart that the white taffeta will be released as scheduled. See you soon, little minx.

I felt a sense of giddiness as I closed out of our text thread and moved onto the next part of my master plan. A quick online search was all it took for me to locate the number for *Blooming Bayne*, Ingrid's florist friend, and dial. Luckily, they were open even with the expo earlier in the day.

"Thank you for calling Blooming Bayne, this is Charlotte. How can I help you?"

"Yes, hi," I stammered. I wasn't anticipating her to be the one to answer. "I need to place an order for a bouquet. Would I be able to pick it up in the morning?"

"Absolutely! If you can be here at eight o'clock, I can have it ready for you by then. What were you thinking?"

"This might sound odd, but can you put together a wildflower bouquet with lavender?" I wasn't sure why I thought my little minx would prefer that, but my gut was positive about it.

"I absolutely can! What name should I put this under?"

"Josh Astor, please. And if this is Ingrid's friend, please don't tell her that I'm getting these. It's a surprise." I was practically begging her and I couldn't even be ashamed of how much I sounded like a child.

"Your secret is safe with me." She paused and I could almost feel her resolve harden through the phone. *"But know this, Joshua, if you hurt her, I am very talented with gardening shears."*

Normally, the threat of the friend wasn't that scary, but for some reason, I believed her. Wes was going to have his hands full if he ever got his head out of his ass and asked her out.

"I expect nothing less. Thank you, seriously. I'll see you tomorrow."

With the flower delivery placed, I worked out my grocery list and placed a pick up order to grab on my way to her place in the morning. I made sure to add everything I would need for either waffles or pancakes.

And, okay fine, maybe an extra can of whipped cream.

It was well past one in the morning. I managed to get caught up on my work, went for an evening run, packed up the kitchen necessities I would need for breakfast, and took a *very* cold shower. I was staring at my ceiling from the comfort of my bed while I tried to figure out how I could convince her to fall in love with me. Out of the countless dates my mother had set me up on, not a single other woman had been able to affect me as much as Ingrid Morgan. I couldn't stop thinking about the way she looked when she was bent over her sketchbook, trying with all her might to ignore the obvious tension and just create something. The look of concentration mixed with frustration was so adorable I just wanted to rile her up a little to see what she would do.

Talking with her was so natural and easy. Even when I thought I would ruin it completely, I could see the teasing light in her eyes. Everything about that woman was intoxicating. When she was busy with brides, I would sneak glances to watch her interact with them and others at her booth. Her work was impeccable and it was clear in the way she held herself that she took pride in her work. There were a couple of brides discussing custom dresses with her and I marveled at the way her eyes lit up as she imagined the dresses just waiting to be brought to life. I wanted to bottle up her joy and carry it around with me. I would do anything to see her light shine constantly.

Sleep continued to evade me before I decided a distraction was needed. I started out with just doing some light research into her on my phone, where the basic information was easy to find. She was 27, the senator's daughter, and ran *Love at the Seam* in Staten Island. I found little to nothing about her and her dad together other than her mom had been gone since she was born, and her father never chose to remarry. I shifted gears and went to her website. Again, it was clear that the amount of talent she carried was immeasurable. I recognized her friends as the models of some of the dresses, but then one listing made me pause and pull out my laptop.

This is a big screen job, I thought to myself as I forced my hands to focus on bringing up her website.

I didn't anticipate seeing Ingrid herself model some of the dresses. Each one she wore had me gasping for air. Her face wasn't in all of them, but I could tell by her curves which ones she was in.

When she got married one day, would it be in one of those? No, something told me she would design her own just for herself. A one of a kind. With pockets, probably.

The more I saw, the stronger I found that I wanted to see that dress. I *needed* to see that dress.

An idea began to form and my hands had a mind of their own as I started researching and scheduling, until I eventually drifted off to sleep with visions of my little minx walking down the aisle.

Five

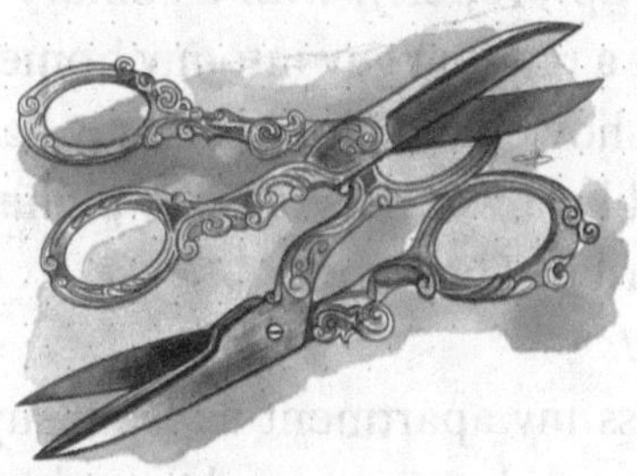

Ingrid

The incessant sound of my alarm had me jolting awake. *Shit.* I grabbed my phone from under my pillow only to be assaulted by it flashing "8:40 AM" loudly in my face.

Fuck, he's going to be here in 20 minutes!

I stumbled out of bed, my leg getting caught in my comforter, as I did a quick sweep of my room to decide what I would wear. I managed to find my favorite lilac sweater, a pair of leggings, my cream fuzzy socks, and then sprinted to the bathroom to take the world's quickest shower.

I gave myself no time at all to contemplate what the hell I was doing. I brushed my teeth while I let the water warm up, spitting in the toilet as my sleep addled brain rushed to go through the motions. Never had I been more grateful for the fact that I waxed, as I managed to shave off (haha) an extra 15 minutes from my shower time by being able to just wash my hair and body.

Dammit, I cursed to myself as I tried to focus on getting clean. I wanted to wake up early so that I had time to style my hair and maybe even get some sketching done while I waited for him. I wanted to wake up properly, with a solitary cup of coffee in peace, before I let a random guy into my home.

I got out of the shower and blow dried my hair just enough so that I didn't look like a wet rat. As I was pulling my socks over my leggings, I heard it. The knock.

Fuck, he's early!

I sprinted across my apartment as I put my deodorant on, tossing it behind me without a second thought on my way to the door. By the time I opened it, I was out of breath and flushed, and not just in regards to my chaotic morning. Standing in front of me was Joshua Astor (the Third), dressed casually in a long sleeve pullover and jeans. He was carrying multiple grocery bags as he leaned casually against my door frame. I tried not to admire the way his arms flexed as he adjusted his grip. When I dragged my gaze up to his, I could see a teasing look in his eye with his own shit eating grin to match. He knew *exactly* how good he looked.

"Good morning, little minx," he said, the grin not leaving his face for a second.

Little minx. There it was again.

I didn't know why, but something about him calling me that made me blush redder than my favorite lipstick. It clearly showed, as the mischievous glint in his eye grew stronger. It looked like he wanted to see what else would make me blush. He leaned over and pushed a stray hair behind my ear as he leaned in to whisper, "Are you going to let me in or will I need to eat right here in the doorway?"

Shivers traveled down my spine as my senses went haywire from the mix of his tobacco vanilla scent and the brush of his lips against my neck as he stood up straight again.

I took a step back as I cleared my throat before I finally said, "Come on in. Sorry for the mess." I looked around my apartment for the first time since waking up. "Shit," I muttered as I realized it was worse than I initially thought. There was fabric draped over one of my chairs next to my sewing table and mannequin, my coffee table was covered in sketches, and yep, there was the deodorant, in the middle of the floor. I winced and looked back at him while he surveyed my living space.

"Is the deodorant a permanent fixture? How often do you trip on that?" He was still smiling like an ass and I could hear the faintest start of a laugh in his tone.

"Honestly, I'm just impressed it landed straight up when I threw it," I admitted with a shrug. I walked over to pick it up and started clearing up the sketches and fabric as he followed me inside. I heard him lock the door behind him and was shocked by how much that simple act meant to me. It was domestic almost, like I could picture him doing it every day in our own home for the rest of our lives, prioritizing our safety.

What the fuck?

I shook off the feeling as I heard him walk further into the living space. "Out of all the times I've thrown random items in a rush, that has to be the first time anything has ever landed so perfectly. Kitchen is over there," I pointed behind him.

My apartment was an open concept plan with the kitchen overlooking the living room, and I may or may not have watched him walk all the way to the island to set the bags down.

Goddamn, he has a nice ass.

I took another glance around and saw that outside of my work, and the deodorant, nothing else seemed to be too outlandish or messy. Luckily, I made sure to do a thorough clean of my kitchen the night prior before I poured over my sketchbook. I loved my space. I took a lot of pride in how homey I made it feel over the years. My kitchen had open shelves with an array of homemade pottery of plates, bowls, and mugs. All of my silverware was thrifted, and I loved that none of it matched. I typically kept a vase of flowers on the island, but I hadn't had a chance to get another bouquet from Char those past couple of weeks.

My living room was equally cozy, with a plush couch covered in throw pillows and a blanket or two. All of my furniture had also been thrifted. I had a bookshelf in the corner by the window next to my wing backed reading chair with one shelf purely dedicated to my travel knick-knacks. I hadn't gone very far, but I also kept any trinkets Desi's parents sent me up there as well.

I followed the sound of his rummaging once I finished picking up the living room so that it looked a little less like a workaholic explosion. He had the bags on the counter and seemed to be looking for something in the cabinets. "I'll go ahead and get the coffee started. How do you like yours?" I moved toward my coffee bar and waited for his answer before I started grinding the coffee beans.

"I like hazelnut vanilla lattes, but I'm not picky. I'll drink whatever." His voice was muffled as he continued to look through my cabinets. Finally, he seemed to have found whatever he was looking for. "Aha! I knew you would have a vase somewhere."

I took a better look at the items he brought in and realized there was a stunning bouquet of wildflowers nestled safely on one of the bags. "Is that lavender in that bundle?" I questioned as I took a closer look at them. They were tied off with a string of twine and I could see the card attached had the signature *Blooming Bayne* logo on it.

Charlotte, you bitch, why didn't you tell me he was coming with flowers?!

"It is. Do you like them?" He looked nervous all of a sudden, his previous confidence melted off of him. It was like he took a wild guess it was my preferred bouquet and was just praying he would get it right. He did.

"They're beautiful. Thank you, Josh," I told him earnestly and with a softness I would give a scared child.

The beam on his face was instant and he let out a breath that he seemed to have been holding since he asked his question. He was looking at me like I held the answers to every question he'd ever asked.

I pointed him in the direction of where to put the groceries as I distracted myself by getting started on the lattes. I kept a fully stocked coffee bar just on the off chance I was ever in the mood for something different, so I was able to make him his preference along with my lavender.

He was putting the last of the groceries away as I placed his latte on the cleared off island before taking a seat on the other side. Once he was done, he turned and looked at me, bracing his arms on the counter between us. He took a sip of his coffee and with an approving nod, he said, "So, the question returns. What are you in the mood for, little minx? Waffles or pancakes?" The smile he wore when he first walked in was back in full force, those previous anxious feelings gone without a trace.

"Hmm." I tapped a finger on my chin. "I'm thinking waffles."

"Waffles it is then. Strawberries and whipped cream, right?" I nodded excitedly causing him to laugh as he then asked, "Do you eat meat? I grabbed some sides as well, but I made sure to get vegan alternatives to be safe." I wasn't sure why, but that took me aback for a second. I did eat meat, but the fact that he went out of his way to be that considerate on the chance that I didn't, might have been the sweetest thing a man had ever done for me.

"I eat meat. Are you always this nice?" I watched as he began taking off his pullover and washing his hands. I had to force myself to listen for his response because *holy hell* his arms were even more toned than I realized. I wondered what those would feel like wrapped around me or pinning me down.

No, bad Ingrid! I mentally chastised myself. *This is just a nice man, here to cook you breakfast and then will probably never see you again.*

"I try to be. Although, I promise, little minx, I have my moments where you may sing a different tune." That mother fucker *winked* at me from over his shoulder. Before I could even respond to that or give it more thought, he continued, "So, tell me, what got you into wedding dress designing? Surely with the father you have, there must've been some pressure to go into politics."

He wasn't wrong, but that was mostly from the public, not my father. I told him as such and then said, "I watched all of the wedding dress shows growing up and couldn't help but notice that the girls like me, and bigger, weren't able to get the dresses they dreamed of because designers would stop at a size 6. I wanted to be sure that not only would I be able to have my own dream dress, but all the other girls like me would as well." I wasn't ashamed of the fact that I was curvy, in fact I loved it. I found all women beautiful and I was a firm believer that the clothes were made to fit you, *not* the other way around.

He watched me closely as I explained all of this to him and I caught him struggling between looking in my eyes and away from my mouth. I could see his gaze heat as he hung on every word, like hearing my passion turned him on.

I wonder what else will make him look at me like that.

"So, I started designing really young. Obviously, the child sketches were pretty lackluster, but as I got older, they turned into more. I went to fashion school so that I could learn more about materials, fabrics, and sewing techniques and over time, I realized I might actually be able to do this. I won't hide away from the fact that my father helped fund my dream and bought the building for me, but it's all in my name now and my business is successful because of my work alone," I continued to explain my journey to him. "Wedding expos, like the one yesterday, are actually what helped turn my dream into a reality. Each bride gets a one of a kind gown, either custom for them or one of the premade options I have downstairs."

"I can tell how hard you've worked for this. I couldn't help but notice you yesterday during the expo and seeing you interact with the brides. I saw your dresses. They're almost as beautiful as their maker, Ingrid. You should be proud." Outside of him reading my name off of my business card the day before, that was the first time he'd called me by my name.

And oh boy, did I love the way it sounded rolling off of his tongue. He made it sound like my name could live in his mouth.

Shaking off the obvious blush, I cleared my throat and turned the topic onto him, instead. "So, Mr. Joshua Astor the Third, tell me, what are your plans? I know you're the COO of *Astor Investments*, but is that your end goal?"

He considered his answer as he began mixing the waffle batter before replying, "The plan is to take over the company completely. My dad has trained me up to take the reins my entire life. Don't get me wrong, I've always had the option to do something different if I wanted to, but I enjoy this work. I'm ready to take over the moment he deems it." I could tell he had more to add, but was hesitating. He took a deep breath as he seemed to reach a conclusion. "There's just one hold up."

I tilted my head as I waited for him to look at me. "Oh?"

"My father wants me to be married first. To show that I can be committed to more than just the business. He wants me to have a life outside of the company, so that I don't get burnt out and end up with regrets later on."

Interesting, it sounded like his father and my own should get together. They could bond over their mutual *"marry off the children"* ideas.

Josh started mixing the batter more aggressively, showing his nerves, as he added, "I don't disagree with him. I'm at a point in my life where I want a family as much as I want the company. It isn't about continuing the legacy or anything like that, I just want to go home at the end of the day and it feel, well, like *home.*"

His hand paused its mixing as his shoulders drooped and his eyes bore into mine. Once again, he was looking at me like I held all the answers. He was looking at me like he hoped, just maybe, *I* would be his home.

And kill me, but I didn't think I hated that idea.

Six

Joshua

*F*uck. Maybe it was a bad idea to tell her all of that. She was going to think I was insane. I'd barely even scratched the surface of what I was hoping would begin the best journey of my life, maybe even *our* lives.

I looked away quickly and kept working on breakfast. If I looked at her and saw that she didn't feel the same way, it would crush me.

The implications were clear, I wanted everything with her.

"You know, I had the same conversation with my dad yesterday at lunch," she mused from her place at the island. "My response to him was pretty similar to yours." I could feel my heart beating faster in my chest, but it wasn't from nervousness.

This might actually work.

I tried to look nonchalant as I poured waffle mix into the waffle maker and flipped the bacon. "Yeah? Is your dad trying to set you up with all of the eligible bachelors in New York? My mom won't stop setting me up on random dates." I didn't feel the need to hide that from her, if anything, it was good information for her to have to fully understand what her could-be mother-in-law would be like. "I had to talk to her last night about putting an end to it."

She laughed and the sound moved through the air and filled my chest with warmth. "No, my dad hadn't tried any of that. However, if he knew that one of New York's top 10 most eligible bachelors were in my apartment cooking me breakfast right now, I know he would lose his mind with glee." *Shit*, I'd forgotten all about that. My mother put me up to it and of course, my face was the one that ended up on the cover.

I winced and tried to play it off like it was from the bacon grease and not the reminder of the article. "You saw that, huh? I swear that article is going to be the death of me. Like it isn't bad enough that I've had to go on dates with women of my mother's choosing, all they see me as is a walking billfold. I promise, while yes I'm rich, I'm much more than that."

I heard her choke on her giggle as her eyes honed in on my arms while I removed one waffle and began pouring the next. She shook her head like she was trying to clear it again.

I promise, little minx, if you say yes, we will have so much fun.

"I believe you, Josh. You went out of your way to get me my favorite flowers from one of my best friend's shops. You got vegan alternative sides just in case I didn't eat meat. I know you're more than what the article alludes to."

Relief bloomed in my chest at her words. We grew into easy conversations as she continued to watch me finish up the breakfast. Once the strawberries were chopped, I loaded up a plate for her with a waffle covered in her favorite fixings and then a side of bacon. She pointed me in the direction of her silverware drawer and I grabbed a fork with a lavender sprig on the stem to place on her plate.

I wanted to test our chemistry a little, so with her plate in one hand and the can of whipped cream in the other, I approached from behind her stool to place her meal in front of her. I tugged on her hair from the base of her skull with my free hand. "Open."

Her gasp was barely audible and I watched as her gaze heated when she looked up at me. Slowly, she opened her mouth further than a slight part of her lips, her tongue peeking out in anticipation. Without breaking eye contact, I sprayed some of the whipped cream into her mouth and watched as she swallowed it. There was the smallest amount of it sitting on the corner of her smile and before she could get it herself, I bent down and licked it off. She tasted like sugar and lavender and my favorite flavor all at once. If the shiver that ran through her told me anything, I could bet that she was covered in goosebumps under her sweater.

Yeah, this will work.

I didn't bother shifting my jeans to hide my erection. I walked back over to where my own waffle still needed to be plated and felt her eyes following me. I was glad she watched. It helped secure for me that she was the one I had been hoping for.

"Go ahead. Eat up," I said as I began to make my own plate. I could almost feel her excitement over the meal radiating through her as she looked down at her waffle. When she finally took a bite, a moan escaped her lips that couldn't go unnoticed. Without missing a beat, I said, "If just my cooking makes that sound escape your mouth, I can't wait to find out what else will."

She shifted on her stool and when I walked back over to sit next to her, I could see her thighs clenching beneath the counter top. I loved knowing my little minx was just as affected as I was.

I didn't want her to be uncomfortable, though, so I shifted gears for the time being. "So, do you agree that I'm the best chef in the city?" I asked with a hint of amusement in my tone. She straightened her back a little more and looked directly at me, eyes glossy and pupils blown. She was fighting the verbal whiplash and instead of commenting on it, I took a bite of my own waffle while I waited for her response.

"I don't know. You'll need to make pancakes next time to truly put it to the test," she finally said.

Okay, I can play that game.

"Oh, I anticipate there will be many *next times* in our future, little minx."

Red the color of roses spread across her cheeks at the pet name. She loved when I called her that, if her reaction was anything to go by.

We went over our plans for the day as we ate our waffles next to each other. It felt comfortable, like we'd done that our entire lives and would for all years to come. She had some work she needed to get done between organizing the information with the brides from the expo and working on her sketches. I, however, had cleared my schedule for the day. I wanted to watch her work, plus I had a proposition for her that I really hoped she would agree to.

The nerves built up higher as the conversation turned into amiable silence. I pushed what was left of my food around on my plate to stop from clenching and unclenching my fist. Glancing at her, I said, "I have a question for you, and before you immediately say no, I ask that you hear me out. I need you to understand that I know this idea is insane. This is outside of anything I've ever done and all I'm asking is that you consider it." The sound of her fork clanking on the table was the only noise in the room as she stared at me.

"Something tells me that whatever you are about to ask is outside of normal first breakfast conversations." She grabbed our dishes and walked over to the sink. I deserved an award for only looking at her ass sway for two seconds instead of the full three that it took for her to go from her seat to the other side of the kitchen. "Go ahead, I'm listening. This just feels like the kind of conversation where I need to have something to do with my hands while I consider whatever scheme is moving around in that brain of yours. You know, I can literally *see* the wheels turning." I couldn't see her face, but I didn't need to in order to know that she was arching a brow at me. As much as I wanted to smack her ass for the attitude, she ultimately wasn't wrong. Hell, if there was something *I* could be doing right then, I would've been.

This is why you have to stop cleaning as you cook, I thought to myself.

I didn't let myself think any longer than it took to take a steadying breath.

"Both of our parents want us to get married. I understand that for you, while the pressure isn't as severe, there is pressure nonetheless. I want to be honest when I tell you, even though my mother has sent me on countless blind dates these past few months, none of them have held a candle to you." I watched as her back moved with the deep inhale she made. "I haven't stopped thinking about you since the moment I saw you at the expo eating wedding cake for breakfast. I can't get you out of my head."

My hands were shaking as I swallowed the lump in my throat as I prepared for what came next. She tilted her head in my direction and I took that as her wanting me to continue.

"Move in with me. For three months."

Her hair fanned out with how hard she turned her head to gawk at me. Her eyes flashed with so many emotions, as she gaped at me. I couldn't count them all, but I definitely saw shock, disbelief, and maybe even a little intrigue as she tried to process my words. She opened her mouth, wanting to interject, but I cut her off before she could.

"Again, I know this is insane. Please, just hear me out. You can move in with me in Manhattan, or I'm even willing to move in here so that you're still close to your shop. Just three months." I was standing now and walking toward her. I forced myself to stop at the edge of the island and not reach for her. "Just enough time to see how compatible we are with each other and if this chemistry I *know* you feel between us is there. If after three months we realize this doesn't work, we can go our separate ways."

I held my breath as she studied me for a moment. Once she turned back to the dishes, I heard her ask, "And if at the end of the three months, we realize it *does* work, what then?"

I anticipated this question. I planned out my response to this exact scenario once I came up with my ludicrous plan.

"If it works, then at the end of the three months, I'll propose. Then I will get to see you in the dress you've always dreamed of. I can't wait to see what you come up with, by the way. I just know you'll create something absolutely gorgeous."

She scoffed as she turned back to me. "Oh, you sound very sure that this is all going to take place. How do I know you aren't just using me to take over your fathers company?"

It was a fair question, even if I was a little hurt by it.

"I won't lie and say that marriage would solve my problem with taking over as CEO, I already told you that it would." I couldn't hold myself back anymore. I needed to touch her. It took two steps for me to get behind her and not even one second for me to wrap an arm around her waist. I pulled her into me until her back was flush against me and shifted her hair away from her neck.

Tilting her head so that my lips grazed the shell of her ear, I murmured, "Ingrid, I've never done this before. I've never thought about doing this before." She shivered as I nipped at her jaw. "You have crawled your way under my skin and no matter how hard I try, I cannot, nor do I want to, get you out. Take a leap with me, let me make you breakfast every morning." I kissed the racing pulse point just below her ear. "Let me show you how much I want this, not because of work, but because I want *you*." I let my teeth graze her neck as I moved my lips back to her ear, nipping at the lobe. "*Please*, little minx."

Her hands had a white knuckle grip on the edge of the sink as she leaned further into my touch, plate forgotten. Wanting more, she pushed up onto her tiptoes to press the curve of her ass firmly against my groin.

I knew she could feel my reaction.

I was counting on it.

She shook her hands in an attempt to quickly dry them and turned in my grip until her front was against mine. I had her completely boxed in, she couldn't leave even if she wanted to, but I was betting that she didn't. Carefully, I felt her fingers crawl up my chest and I shamelessly flexed just a little so that she could get a feel for what was hiding beneath my shirt. Still on her tiptoes, she leaned closer to my face as one hand gripped my shirt while the other snaked its way into my hair.

B. CASTLE

Her lips a breath away from mine, she whispered, "I don't like diamonds."

And then I kissed her like my life depended on it.

Seven

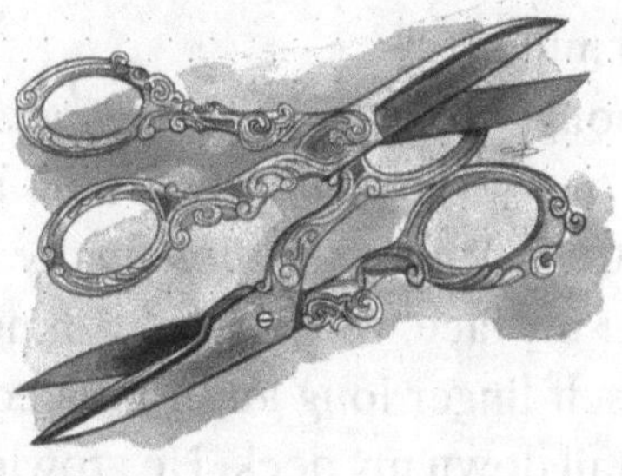

Ingrid

His hands gripped me possessively with one on my side and the other back at the base of my head, tangling in my hair, as he pulled me deeper into the kiss. His tongue darted out to skim the seam of my lips and I couldn't deny him entry if my life depended on it. He kissed me like he was starving for me, like he wanted to swallow every breath and moan I gave him just so he could keep them to himself.

This was crazy.

This was insane.

I didn't let myself think about all of the ways this was a bad idea or how it was a recipe for disaster with either of us ending up hurt. All I did was feel.

I felt my pulse in my neck as his lips migrated to suck just below my ear.

I felt my breath stutter as I used my grip in his hair to push him deeper into me.

I felt my skin pebble as his hands gripped my ass to hoist me into his arms, my legs wrapped around his waist.

All I could do was hold on.

He started moving us and I tugged on his hair to drag his mouth back up to mine.

I was right, I thought to myself, *very tuggable, indeed.*

He carried me over to my open bedroom and lowered me down to the mattress. When our lips finally broke apart, his eyes bounced over my face, wide and gleaming, mouth parted. He didn't let himself linger long and I inhaled his scent as he started kissing a trail down my neck. He growled at my sweater being in the way and I could see him fisting my comforter to stop himself from ripping off the offending material.

"So, what will it be, little minx? My place or yours?" He asked, like he wasn't distracting me to high heaven with his mouth.

I tried my best to really think through any reasoning before I eventually responded, "Mine. I have zero desire to worry about commute times to get to work everyday. Plus it's easier with all of my supplies." His weight shifted as he finally let go of the blanket before I felt his fingers tease the hem of my sweater and he started to drag it up my sides.

Instead of continuing upward, he moved his hands back down toward my hips, leaving feather light touches along my sides as he did. I squirmed with impatience beneath him and he chuckled in my ear and murmured, "I figured as much, I already have people packing up a portion of my stuff to bring over here this afternoon. I would bring it all, but I did some research last night and figured there wouldn't be enough space for everything. That'll be something we'll need to work out later down the line."

His lips were back on mine before I could muster a response, the taste of strawberries and hazelnuts flooding my mouth. His hands moved higher again under my sweater and when I could feel the tips of his fingers brush against my bare breasts, he abruptly sat up, eyes even wider than they were before as he stared directly into my soul.

Best part about oversized sweaters? It's not always obvious when one is braless.

"Off." Pointing at my sweater, his eyes lingered on where he knew there was nothing beneath. "Now, little minx. Don't make me tell you again."

I'd never been as unsteady as I was when I pushed myself up into a kneeling position as he stood next to the bed, towering over me. Slowly, I peeled my sweater off and shivered at the sudden chill. I watched his pupils blow the moment I was bare for him. He almost seemed to be in a trance as his gaze followed the rise and fall of my breasts with each breath I took. Before I lost my nerve, I reached out for his t-shirt and said, "Your turn."

Without missing a beat, he removed his shirt one handed and tossed it aside to let me get my fill. Toned didn't even *begin* to describe him. If he asked me to join him in the gym, I would only do so on the pretense of being able to just sit and watch him. It was clear even from my position on the mattress that his shoulders were equally as impressive. I trailed my gaze along each line of muscle as they just kept going down, *down*, into a perfect v that dipped below the waistline of his jeans. His erection was pressing so hard against the zipper, I was worried he was in pain. At least, that's what I told myself as I reached for the buckle on his belt before he stopped me by grabbing my wrist.

"Not yet, it's my turn now." With two fingers, he nudged me in the shoulder to get me to lay back down on the bed. He grabbed my legs from under me to pull them straight so he could fit himself between them. His mouth was back on my neck faster than I could blink. One hand was pressing my hip firmly into the bed while the other was teasing my nipple, circling and pinching the bud between two knuckles causing an involuntary moan to slip out. I felt his lips move down the length of my throat, not kissing, just letting them drag across my skin. Ever so often, his teeth would graze a little, making me jump. "You did it again. I know I promised that I wouldn't delay the taffeta, but I hope you'll forgive me if I do. My plans for today are now to find each and every way to make that sound come out of you again." As if he already knew that I would try to protest, he sucked my other nipple into his mouth while tugging again on the opposite.

"Please, Josh," I gasped as his fingers moved from my breast to join his other hand at my hips. I wrapped my fingers back into his hair in an attempt to push his head further south.

I needed *more*.

Luckily, he followed the direction I was desperately trying to give him and when his mouth made it the waistband of my leggings, he looked up. "I'm clean. I got tested last week and funny enough, I got the results back yesterday." Desire swam in his eyes as he waited for me to say something. He needed this as much as I did.

"Same here. C-clean, I mean. And I'm on birth control. Just got my last shot a couple of weeks ago." I deserved a pat on the fucking back, a gold star, *and* a cookie for being able to manage responding at all, let alone being thorough enough to get the point across. He seemed to agree, because before I could even brace myself, he grabbed onto my leggings and tugged them down in one fell swoop. In my rush to get ready, I went without underwear entirely. I knew the moment that fact registered to him, I would be in for it.

"You mean to tell me, that all morning you've been walking around with *nothing* underneath all of this?" I nodded and chewed on my bottom lip as he continued removing my leggings and fuzzy socks off of me. "You couldn't put on panties, but you could remember the socks?" He looked caught between amused and intrigued by the fact, like he couldn't quite believe how seriously I took my warmth and comfort in my barely awake state.

The moment my body was free of the confines of my clothes, he nestled his face between my thighs and began lazily kissing them as he positioned them over his broad shoulders. "Now that I know this fun little fact about you, I hope you realize that commando is the only way you will be going from now on. Especially while we're home." My breath caught at him calling my apartment *home*, but before I could think too hard about it, he bit down on my inner thigh before his hands pulled me by my hips closer to his face. "I want you ready like this every damn day from now until the end, little minx."

Spreading my legs further apart, he moved his hands so that his thumbs could spread my pussy out for him to see. I had been turned on since the moment I saw him at my front door. I already knew how soaked I was. He licked his lips while he moved one hand around to swipe a finger through my wetness from opening to clit. He groaned as he sucked it into his mouth. "Of course you taste as sweet as you look."

He snaked his arm back under my leg and placed his thumb back to where I was squirming, desperate for some friction, and outlined my clit teasingly. I could feel his eyes on my face as he waited for a reaction of any kind. Thrusting my hips up, I silently pleaded with him for *more*. His mouth turned to my other thigh as I felt him *finally* touching me. He sucked on my thigh, no doubt leaving a mark while he continued to play with my clit.

I felt his other hand move under so that he could position his index finger at my entrance while he nipped at the sensitive point on my inner thigh. When he bit down harder, eliciting an even louder moan to escape from my lips, he entered me.

Fucking me with his hand, he unlatched from my thigh and began moved his mouth higher to suck on my clit while adding a second finger. I could feel my orgasm already brewing in the base of my spine as I started arching off the bed. He was showing me absolutely no mercy as his teeth gently bit down on my swollen clit just as he curled his finger just right, pressing onto my g-spot like he owned it. He never took his eyes off of me and I knew he felt my body start to coil tighter and tighter around him. Popping his mouth off of me, he said, "Now, little minx. Let me hear you."

My orgasm ripped through me as I screamed out his name, not needing any further permission for the bowstring that became my body to snap. He didn't ease up, his mouth back on my clit and his hand still driving into me as he prolonged my release. I was beyond keeping even a modicum of composure as I moaned nonsensical words and noises.

As my muscles began to relax, I felt him shift off of the bed as he got up to remove his buckle and jeans. I sat back up and repositioned myself into my kneeling position as I waited for him to fully address, doing my best to stay upright. He was standing again beside the bed, and I was met with his cock right at my eye level. Licking my lips, I began to inch forward, absolutely dying to get a taste as I saw precum dripping from his head. I never thought I would think that a penis was beautiful, but all I wanted to do was worship the one in front of me. He was built like a God in every aspect of the word and I couldn't fucking *wait* have him inside of me.

Before I could give him the best head of his life, his hand was back on the base of my skull, tugging harder so that I was looking at him with what I assumed was a pout on my face. I held eye contact as I reached for his thighs and pulled him closer to me.

"You had your turn. Now it's mine," I said in a matter of fact tone. Without letting go of me, he watched as I took his cock into my mouth, licking the precum right up before taking him deep into my throat. When I swallowed around his length, I could tell he was refraining from fucking my face as his grip tightened further.

"Fuck, Ingrid," he groaned, stilling himself to let me work. "You look so fucking perfect with my cock in your mouth, pretty girl."

I worked my head up and down, making sure to swirl my tongue and graze him with my teeth just enough to watch the shiver course through his body. I could tell he was getting close, so I reached up to cup his balls as I moved to take him all the way down to the base once more.

Before I could continue, I was yanked off, a string of my saliva the only thing still connecting my mouth to his cock.

"No. Bad, little minx. As much as I would love to watch you swallow every drop of my come, that is not where I'll be finishing this morning." I watched as he backed up, working out where he wanted me. He moved onto the bed, his legs spread with his heels tucked underneath him, similar to the kneel I was in, and leaned back against my headboard. Crooking one finger, he said, "Crawl."

Without a moment's hesitation, I turned to crawl just as he asked until I was close enough for him to reach me and I was straddling his lap. He kept his hands on my hips as he held me hovering just over him, so close I could feel him at my entrance. He kissed my collar bone, worshipping me further as he slowly lowered me down onto him. I moaned his name as I felt him getting deeper and deeper until I was flush against him. He let out a shaky breath as one arm wrapped around my waist, hand back in my hair. I placed my hands on the headboard behind him, already knowing he wasn't going to stay gentle.

As he let me adjust to his size, he whispered almost too softly for me to hear, "You are the most beautiful woman I have ever known. I'm going to keep you." He didn't let me respond before he began thrusting into me, swallowing my moan with a devouring kiss.

Eight

Joshua

I didn't show any mercy as I continued to thrust into her from our position. She found the rhythm I set almost immediately and began meeting me at every stride, riding my cock like the pro I knew she would be.

"*Fuuuuuck*, little minx," I groaned into her throat, pulling her hair to give me the access I needed. "You feel so fucking incredible."

I was going to live between her thighs. She would never know another in her bed, or any other for that matter. Now that I had gotten a taste, I wouldn't give her up for anything. The next three months were just the beginning. If this was any indication, I would be proposing once all was said and done.

Still wrapped around her, I lifted up on my knees and began to lower her back onto the mattress. Without breaking our momentum, I untangled my fingers from her hair and moved my hand down to her thigh, lifting it up and over my shoulder to take her even deeper. Her gasp in my mouth almost made me come undone, but I needed one more from her before I would allow myself any release. I needed her to not think about anything else outside of us by the time we were done. I needed to be imprinted so deep into the marrow of her bones that she wouldn't be able to rethink our agreement.

That was probably super unhealthy, but I didn't give a fuck. I needed her to be just as consumed with me as I was with her.

I pulled my mouth away from her to sit up just enough to give her a break. I wanted her next orgasm to be with mine and if I let her come right then, I wouldn't last. I looked down between us and watched as I glided in and out of her.

"Look how perfect you take me, Ingrid," I crooned as I continued my thrusts. Grabbing her other thigh, I brought her legs together and set them on the same shoulder. Her pussy tightened more than I anticipated and I grit my teeth as I plunged deeper into her. I could tell she was close, my name effortless on her lips, her body unable to hide how much she was desperate for another release.

Fine. You win, little minx.

"So."

Thrust.

"Fucking."

Thrust.

"Perfect."

Thrust.

"Come for me again, little minx. Let me feel you squeeze me." For good measure, I pinched her clit between my knuckles as I leaned forward until our faces were almost touching, legs still over my shoulder. With that, my girl *screamed*.

If I thought she was tight before, nothing, and I mean nothing, was a match for the feeling of her coming around me. I knew she would feel incredible, but what I wasn't expecting was for me to lose my vision as her orgasm wrung my own out of my cock without mercy. I kept pumping into her as my release spilled out of me before I spread her legs and brought them back down.

I knew I was heavy. As hard as I tried not to collapse on top of her, I still ended up doing exactly that. I didn't have a choice, I'd never come that hard before.

She squirmed beneath me and I could faintly hear her voice say, "Mmash woff mcrenople."

A laugh escaped before I could stop myself and I managed to roll off of her, pulling out in the process. I gently swept the hair out of her eyes and tucked it behind her ear. "What was that?"

"That was incredible," she said, all big eyed and sweat glistening on her body. I watched as she rolled to face me.

"It was," I murmured absently as her fingers trailed along my skin. We didn't say anything else for a long while, just content to share breaths and stare into each other.

I was starting to drift off, suddenly exhausted, when I heard her whisper, "Please don't break my heart. I'll take the leap with you, just please don't hurt me."

She looked so nervous and shy in that moment and I wrapped an arm around her waist to tuck her into my chest before placing what I hoped was a reassuring kiss on her head. "I wouldn't dream of it, little minx. Not in a million lifetimes. I promise to worship the ground you walk in until the day I die." I felt a single tear drip onto my chest and I pulled away. Wiping it carefully off of her cheek with my thumb, I grabbed her chin to tilt her mouth up for a kiss. "Come on, let's go get cleaned up."

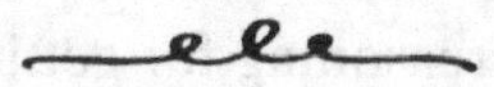

After we took a shower, where I gave her the best scalp massage of her life, if I said so myself, we went to the living room where I watched as she grabbed her bag and began pulling out her folder. I couldn't help but see the beak of a magazine underneath as though it was wedged between her sketchbook and the folder.

"Little minx, what's that?" Her cheeks flushed that brilliant red once more at my question. I held a hand out and said, "Bring it here." I had a feeling I knew what it was, but I needed to tease her at least a little. She hesitated before handing me her messenger bag, but once she caved, I snatched it playfully before she could second guess herself. I carefully extracted the magazine, and yep, there was my face. I pretended to be surprised as I looked at her and asked, "How long have you had this?"

Popping her hip out, she rolled her eyes and said, "Oh hush. I grabbed it on my way to lunch with my dad after the expo yesterday. Don't tell me you're worried I only gave you my number because I thought you looked cute on glossy paper." We would get back to the eye rolling later, even if the sight had my dick twitching again.

"Well, how am I supposed to know you don't just like me for my retouched good looks?" I could see her getting riled up. Her nose was doing the scrunchy thing it did when she concentrated and her eyes were glaring daggers at me.

Her features only looked like that for a moment before they smoothed over and a smile that would destroy in a board meeting appeared. "You know, I'm in a magazine as well. I could accuse you of the same crime." I swallowed as she cocked her head to the side. "How am I to assume your mother hasn't been reading wedding magazines religiously these past few months and you didn't see *me* on the cover? Although, mine isn't retouched." Given her reasoning for getting into her career, I wasn't shocked by what she was saying. And while she was right that my mother *had* been doing exactly that, I hadn't paid any attention to them. Now, I was wishing I had.

"Let me see," I said, the fake tiff forgotten. "Show me. Please."

She moved across the room to her bookshelf and pulled the magazine off without needing to search for it. I could see the glee in her eyes from knowing she won as she stalked back over. She took a seat next to me on the couch and went to pass it over. Before she did, she stopped herself. "Are your hands clean? This is very important documentation and I'll be very upset if you smudge it." I couldn't help but laugh as I reached over to grab her waist and pulled her onto my lap.

"How about this, I'll let you hold it the whole time while I look from right here," I murmured in her ear as I buried my face into her neck. I could feel the shiver race down her spine as she melted into my touch, magazine falling to her lap in her distraction.

There she was, right there on the cover. She was wearing a cream dress that pushed her perfect tits sky high. It hugged her in a corseted bodice that dropped into a cloud of tulle. I swallowed around a lump in my throat as I studied the image. The photographer captured her smile mid laugh, her beauty on full display. I kissed her neck again as I muttered, "Is this what I can expect to see walking toward me?"

She leaned further into my touch and said just as softly, "I guess you'll have to wait and see."

Just as I was tilting her head to face mine so I could kiss her the way I wanted, my phone vibrated in my pocket. She let out a sharp gasp as I realized she was sitting directly over it, likely feeling the vibration all the way on her clit. I gently picked her up and moved her to sit next to me so I could dig my phone out of my pocket. Unlocking it, I saw I had a notification from the moving company, letting me know they were at her place.

I let her know what they said and as I was walking toward her front door she said, "Wow, you weren't kidding when you said you just knew this would work out." She followed me as we made it to the door.

"I was fully prepared to pay them to turn right back around, if needed. Something told me you would take the leap, though."

We let the movers in and I helped them navigate the boxes to their respective areas. I didn't bring any of my furniture, knowing she likely wouldn't have the space and only brought a few of my kitchen needs. Other than that, I just asked for a box of my records, my record player, and enough clothes to get me through the season. Once the three months came to an end, we would need to discuss the living arrangements further, but that was a problem for future us.

Once the movers left, I gave her a kiss and let her get to work while I unpacked. There wasn't much space for my suits, but I was able to make it work with a touch of rearranging, careful not to disrupt her flow too much. I was able to find space for my kitchen items and determined the record player was going on the other side of her book shelf furthest away from her reading chair.

When I was finally done, I grabbed my laptop and took a seat on the couch to get caught up on emails. It didn't take long for me to get distracted, as out of the corner of my eye, I could see her concentration face back in full force.

"Little minx," I started, without glancing away from my screen. "If you insist on looking that adorable while you work, we're going to need to come up with a plan for where I can get my own work done away from you."

Without missing a beat or looking away from her sketch-book, she responded, "There's a perfectly suitable island with seating right behind you." I was looking at her then, my work for the day be damned.

Closing my laptop completely, I walked over to where she was at her desk. Bracing my hands on either side of her, caging her in, I kissed her cheek. "What are you working on?" She was sketching away, the dress taking form right before my eyes. Above her sketchbook, she had a client order form sitting there with descriptions on what the bride was looking for. Reading it, I could see that the bride wasn't overly descriptive and seemed to give Ingrid room for creative control. They must've been one of the brides from the expo that I saw chatting with her.

"This bride is wanting an ethereal look. Her and her partner are big *Lord of the Rings* fans, so she wants to look like a woodland elf," she explained. Focusing back on the sketch, I could see the influence. The dress was flowing in a multitude of directions and she was starting on what appeared to be a cap as opposed to a veil.

"It's beautiful. Just like you," I muttered, pressing a kiss to the top of her head. She shooed me away with a wave of her hand.

"No distracting, Joshua Astor, you've already thrown me off kilter enough for one day," she said with fake annoyance in her voice. As I leaned back up, I heard her stomach start to grumble.

Ah yes, it was time to use some of the other items from my grocery run.

I kissed her cheek one last time and started to walk away. She never lost focus as her hunger was clearly trying to win over. "How about this, I'll make us some lunch and you have to take a break long enough to eat it, and then I won't bother you the whole time I am sitting right there," I pointed to the island, "getting my own work done." She looked up at me then, and her eyes sparkled.

"Okay, I like that idea! Let's aim to be done working for the day by 5. If I let myself pour over these longer than that, the dresses start to get weird," she said.

While I laughed at my little workaholics antics, I made a mental note to make sure I reminded her to take care of her needs from time to time.

Nine

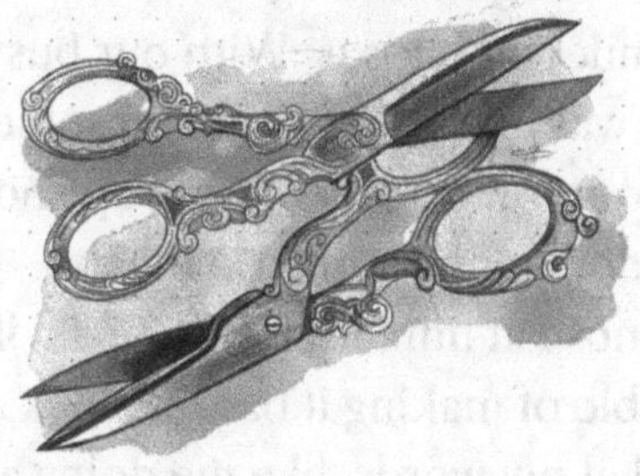

Ingrid

Josh had been living with me for three days and as much as I didn't want to admit it, everything had been amazing. I did get breakfast every day, just like he promised, as well as dinner. He cleaned up after himself. Hell, he didn't even snore.

He didn't always need to go into the office so some days he worked at the counter. It seemed he only needed to go in when there were bigger meetings, so for the most part, we got to spend our days together. He managed to find a local gym within running distance, which was perfect since that was apparently a daily ritual.

On Saturday, I went to go see the girls for brunch down the street and to say I was nervous would have been an understatement. I hadn't told them about everything that had happened after the expo, and I had no clue how they would take the news. I'd always been a little impulsive and spontaneous, but our arrangement definitely took the cake.

Before I left, Josh pulled me in one last time and gave me a kiss. "Have fun with the girls and let me know if you need me to pick you up after the mimosas," he said, tapping my nose. I told him about how the girls and I got together once a month for brunch and bottomless mimosas. With our busy schedules, our Saturday girl's day was important to us and something we always blocked our time out for, usually closing up shop on those days just in case we ended up drinking too much.

Scrunching my nose at him, I said, "Fine, I will. Even though I am perfectly capable of making it back a block and a half on my own." He frowned at my words, like me doing anything without his assistance was just plain rude. He knew I was independent, he just wanted to lend a hand when he could.

"Go, behave yourself, little minx." He swatted my ass as I turned back toward the door. "I'll see you later." He left a lingering kiss and then I was on my way to see my two best friends, praying they wouldn't kill me after I told them my news.

When I made it to *Over Easy*, I spotted Char and Desi already waiting for me at our usual booth. Their faces lit up and then both of them immediately tilted their heads to the side as if they could already tell something was up. It was almost comical how in sync all three of us were the moment we were put into a room together.

I took my seat next to Desi and got started pouring my first mimosa, pointedly ignoring the looks they were both giving me.

"So, what? No hello? Just gonna breeze past the fact that something is clearly going on and pour yourself a drink?" Char started. I narrowed my eyes at her. She may not have known exactly what was going on, but she sold Josh a bouquet of flowers for me. However, I wasn't going to be the one to mention it.

"I don't know what you're talking about, Char." I turned to Desi, "Hello my beautiful best friend." I looked back at Char, "And hello to my other beautiful best friend. How was your week after the expo?" I heard Desi snort a laugh and Char was looking at me like she couldn't tell if Josh actually showed up with the flowers. Please, who else would he have gotten wildflowers with lavender for? "Have you two been busy at all?"

Desi seemed to be okay with me changing the subject. "Yeah, it's been a fairly normal week for me. You know how it gets this close to the holidays..." She trailed off as she looked between me and Char, picking up that something was happening seeing as Char hadn't stopped staring. "Okay, what the hell is going on with you two right now?"

"Did he hurt you?" Char asked, without missing a beat. "I threatened him with my gardening shears if he hurt you. Did he?" I downed my mimosa and started pouring my next. The girls had already ordered for me, and the waiter appeared with our plates before I had a chance to respond.

"Wait, Ingrid, have you seen Josh again?" Desi asked while I was mid bite of my eggs benedict. I knew once I started this conversation, it would be awhile before I would eat, so I wanted at least one bite while my food was still warm. I set my fork down and looked at both of them, taking another sip of my mimosa to prepare myself for the bomb I was about to drop.

"Okay, both of you chill. Start eating and as you do, I'm going to tell you everything. No interrupting. Chew slowly, because I am not taking questions until the end, and eating will help keep your mouths full enough to avoid trying." They both looked at me like I was insane. Oh, if they only knew just how much. "I'm serious."

Once they both nodded in reluctant agreement, I started from the beginning and told them everything that happened after the expo up until then. Well, *almost* everything. They would ask how he was in bed, I was sure, but I wasn't saying anything unless they did. They both sat there silently eating to respect my request to wait to throw questions at me. There were a few almost spit takes and chokes, but they made it through without interrupting and that's all I could ask. Once I finished getting them up to speed, I downed my mimosa again and poured a third. Unsurprisingly, Char was the first to speak.

"So, let me make sure I'm understanding correctly." She paused to set down her fork. "He made you breakfast, you both got to know one another some, and now he lives with you. In your apartment. Where he's planning to stay for at least three months and then he might *propose*."

I nodded, urging my hands not to betray how nervous I was for their reactions. "Yep, that about sums it up."

It was Desi's turn to say something. "Ingrid, I love you. You know I love you. What the fuck are you doing?" I expected that. I asked myself that question at least once a day, and no matter how much I was living it, it was still difficult to wrap my head around.

"I took a leap," I shrugged." I don't know how to explain it. We just *work*. He was considerate enough to move to the island so that I wouldn't have to learn how to commute back and forth every day. He never forgets to lock the door. He loves watching me work and seeing how passionate I am about what I do. Not to mention, have you seen him?" This got a laugh out of them both

Okay, maybe they'll come around.

Finishing off my third mimosa, I got started on my fourth, the drinks making it way easier to talk about it all.

"Who would've thought, Ingrid Morgan ending up with New York's most eligible bachelor, Joshua Astor the Third," Char said, sounding impressed.

"Are you happy?" I turned to look at Desi and saw the concern written on her face. I loved both of them so much, I knew if either of them were to tell me this was where their lives were going, I would be just as confused and worried.

I nodded as enthusiastically as I could, not because I was trying to convince her, but because my answer was as genuine as the sky was blue. "I am. I really am."

We moved on to other topics while I finished eating my own breakfast, cold as it was, and continued drinking our mimosas. After a couple more hours, all three of us were sufficiently drunk and ready to leave before we ended up banned from our favorite brunch spot. I pulled out my phone to text Josh as having him walk me back didn't sound like too bad of an idea. Before I could send the message, Desi snatched my phone out of my hand.

"Ooo, are you texting Joshy? Here, allow me." I saw her rapidly typing and before I could stop her, let alone see what she wrote, she pressed send. Snatching my phone back, I swayed a little as I read what she sent.

> On our way back now Joshypoooo!!!!! See u sooooon!

Oh, for fuck's sake.

Before I could warn Josh that my phone was hijacked, he sent a response.

Josh

> Can't wait to figure out which one of you sent this message

Desi. We're on our way back now, apparently they are joining

Oh boy, guess I should put some clothes back on…

Just then, Char snatched my phone, read what he sent and cackled like a crazy person. "Seems Desi and I are a couple of cockblockers. Let's go ladies!" She clicked my phone off, shoved it back into my pocket before looping an arm around each of us. Together, we marched back to my apartment singing *I Do, I Do, I Do, I Do, I Do* by ABBA loudly and off key.

By the time we made it into the apartment, stumbling through the door, I was disappointed to see him fully dressed in the same outfit he had on earlier. He chuckled at the pout on my face and at the girls falling into the room behind me, laughing as they did so.

"Oh Joshypoo," Desi sang. "We're home!"

"I can see that," he mused as he walked over and pulled me in for a kiss then bent down to whisper in my ear, "How much did you have to drink, little minx?" I closed my eyes as I relished in his brief touch before he pulled away and headed toward the kitchen. When I opened my eyes, I saw both girls staring at me, jaws to the floor.

"What?"

Char snapped her jaw shut. "Nothing. I see it now. This'll work just fine."

They both walked into the room, approving smiles lighting up both of their faces and I felt myself a much needed sigh of relief. Once Desi spotted the record player, she immediately started *oohing* and *aahing* as she looked through his vinyl collection to pick what she wanted to listen to.

Josh was walking back over to where we each were, as I was still standing at the door while Char had officially plopped down onto the sofa. He handed us each a bottle of water, stepping behind me to close and lock the front door. He took my coat off of me and hung it on the coat rack before placing his hand at the small of my back to walk us to the bar stools. He didn't have me sit like I thought he would, instead taking a seat himself and bringing me to lean between his spread thighs, arm secured around my waist to keep me to him.

"There's some Fleetwood Mac in there, I believe," he said to Desi, who was still looking through his selection. She seemed to have spotted it right as he mentioned it and immediately put it on. "Are you two joining us for dinner? I was planning on making lasagna."

"Well, I wasn't planning on it, but I am now," Char drunkenly announced from her place on the sofa.

"Sounds good to me!" How Desi managed to even respond, I would never know given the fact she was dancing like Stevie Nicks in the corner. She stopped suddenly, wobbling a little as she spun herself dizzy, before adding, "Oh, we should play a game!"

"Yes!" I clapped my hands together and pulled Josh's arm off of me, much to his displeasure, as I ran over to the hall closet that housed all of my board games. Looking over my selection, I reached up to grab Pictionary. Stretching onto my tiptoes, I heard Josh and the girls laughing behind me.

"Baby, stop before you hurt yourself," Josh laughed. He picked me up and plopped me down next to Char on the couch. I crossed my arms and made a face. "Don't scrunch your nose at me. What game did you want?"

I huffed, "Pictionary, please!" When he brought it back over and started setting it up, he looked up to see my face still scrunched. He gave me a quizzical look. "You don't call me baby."

His eyes softened and a small smile graced his lips. "You're right, little minx, I'm sorry." His smile grew to match my own and he continued setting up our game. When Desi finally sat down on my other side, he gave us each a pointed look before saying, "Drink your water, then we can play."

I felt Desi lean in closer to me as she started to open her water bottle, "Yeah, you'll be just fine. I'm happy for you." She kissed me on the cheek and began drinking her water. Char and I followed suit, all doing what we could to sober up so we could kick each other's asses in Pictionary.

Ten

Joshua

"**B**ird's nest!"
        "Silly string!"
"Clump of hair!"
    I watched as Ingrid was aggressively drawing arrows to... *What the hell is that?* The girls were mostly sober and normal as the evening went on and I was in the kitchen cooking dinner. Luckily, I always made enough for leftovers the next day, so Charlotte and Desiree staying for dinner wasn't that big of a deal. Once I put the lasagna in the oven, I made my way over to the girls, slinging the kitchen towel over my shoulder.
    I tilted my head to the side and squinted as I looked closer at her drawing, finally realizing what she was trying to do. "Noodles," I said and watched as Ingrid jumped up, clapping her hands together as she squealed. I felt Desiree's and Charlotte's

glares on me along with the sounds of their yells calling me a cheater. Shrugging, I took a seat in Ingrid's reading chair and held my hand out for her to come over to me.

She plopped right down on my lap, and I took the opportunity to bury my face in her neck, inhaling her lavender espresso scent. "Feeling better?" I whispered in her ear. I felt her head nod against me as she pressed further into my chest. "Good. After dinner, it's time for them to go home. I've been aching to rip that dress off of you since you left with it on." I watched as her cheeks flushed before I gave her a light kiss on her neck and released her so she could go back to her friends. On my way back to the kitchen, I heard the girls muttering to one another behind me. I noticed Ingrid out of the corner of my eye as she started packing the game back up, seemingly trying to hide the blush that creeped up her neck. While I was cleaning the side of the kitchen facing the living room, I saw Ingrid make pointed eye contact with me at the hall closet just before she jumped to put the game back on the top shelf.

Oh, so you want to play that *game tonight. Fair enough, little minx.*

Once dinner was done, the girls all came to sit at the island while I dished out a plate for each of us, giving Ingrid her lavender fork, as always.

"This looks delicious, Josh!" Desiree said as she eyed her plate, turning it occasionally to see where she wanted to grab the first bite.

"It is," Charlotte admitted around a bite she had already taken. "Thanks for the food."

Ingrid and I chuckled at their antics, her already being used to my cooking at that point. As we all settled into our meals, I could feel the interrogation brewing.

"So, we've heard it from her, but now it's your turn to explain," Charlotte started. She had this look in her eye that I knew was likely the same look she had when she threatened me with her gardening shears. "What made you think all of this would be a good idea?" She asked as she made a move with her fork in the air to emphasize her question.

"Char, cut him some slack," Desiree pleaded, offering me an apologetic smile. "Come on, we can see how much he clearly cares about her. He gave her the lavender fork for crying out loud."

Ah, so I had *been right about the fork*, I thought to myself triumphantly. I smirked at Ingrid, throwing her a wink.

"It's a fair question," I responded. "I'd be shocked if you two didn't seem concerned. I know this is a lot to take in. Believe me, when I initially thought up my plan, I didn't really know what I was doing either." If I was going to earn their trust, I had to be honest with them. These two clearly meant the world to Ingrid, and I'd made a promise not to hurt her.

"When Wes pointed you out," I gestured to Charlotte with my fork, "I remember seeing the three of you just laughing, eating wedding cake for breakfast. He didn't mention which one of you three he was interested in at first, and I remember being so nervous he was going to say Ingrid. Luckily, he was looking at you." I could see Charlotte's face light up at the mention of that so before she could say anything, I quickly got out, "No, I'm not getting in the middle of it with you two. He's a grown man, if he's going to ask you out, he needs to do it on his own. I know he wants to, just give him some time." I waited for her to nod in acceptance of the boundary I was laying out. When she did, she waved her hand, urging me to continue.

"Listen, I know that all of this is crazy. Ingrid and I both know that. I'm tired of my mom trying to be the one to set me up with a wife when I want to find the love of my life on my own. I've never felt the kind of joy, partnership, or trust like I do with Ingrid. In the short time that we've known each other, I'm already completely wrapped around her finger, in case you couldn't already tell. I'll protect her, cherish her, and treat her with the love and respect all three of us know she deserves." I looked between the two of them as I made another vow, "I promise."

Desiree and Charlotte both chanced a look at each other, then at me and Ingrid before finally, they both nodded in approval. I could see the tears swimming in Ingrid's eyes as we all returned to our plates.

After dinner, the girls each kissed my little minx on the cheek goodbye with promises to talk soon before they walked out the door. As I hand washed the dishes, I felt her come up behind me and just lean into my back, wrapping me in a hug.

"Thank you," she muttered, her voice so quiet, I had to strain to hear it. "It meant a lot to me that you asked them to stay for dinner. I know the three of us can be a lot when we're together."

Drying my hands off, I turned around and grabbed the hair from the base of her head before pulling hard enough to make her look at me. "I'll do anything if it means hearing your laugh and seeing you smile like I got to today. I like them. They seem to really love you."

She smiled up at me, big and bright, before leaning in to give me a kiss. "They do."

I bent into a squat as I grabbed the backs of her thighs before lifting her up into my arms. She wrapped her legs around my waist and giggled my name into my neck. "Now, if I remember correctly, you and I have plans of our own this evening." I carried her over to the bedroom and plopped her right into the center of the bed. She was wearing a knee length sweater dress that, once again, hugged each of her curves perfectly. Yanking it up and over her head, I made good on my whispered promises from earlier.

Waking up the following Monday, I quickly set out on my morning run before heading back to shower and get dressed in my suit for work. I wouldn't be able to make her breakfast before I left, so I wrote her a note apologizing and placed it with some cash for her to get breakfast at the coffee shop across the street.

Could she pay for it herself? Yes. Did I care? Not really.

Getting in the car, I began the commute to the office. As I was getting on the ferry, my stereo alerted me to an incoming call. Once I saw it was Carlisle Du Pont, our CFO and my other best friend, I quickly answered it.

"Hey man, I'm headed to the office now. Everything okay?"

"Where the hell have you been? I stopped by the penthouse last night hoping to see you for a couple of drinks, but you weren't there. When I went inside, it looked like somebody robbed you of the most random shit!"

I could hear the concern in his voice as he told me about the random items in the kitchen, records, clothes, and toiletries all missing from my apartment. He and Wes both had a key to my place and vice versa. It was useful whenever one of us needed to crash somewhere or if we ever needed a house sitter.

"Sorry about that. I guess we haven't really talked this week, have we?" I rubbed the back of my neck as I realized it was now *my* turn to tell my friends about my crazy plan. "Hang on, let me add Wes to the call. I don't want to explain this twice."

I added Wes to the call, who answered on the third ring.

"What?" he grumbled, and I immediately felt like shit because he was not one for early mornings.

"Hey, I have you and Carlisle on the line. I need to talk to you both about something."

"Yeah, man. Josh got robbed!" Carlisle hollered, effectively startling Wes into full consciousness.

"What do you mean? What did they take?" I could hear the concern in Wes's voice loud and clear along with the rustle of what I could assume was his bed spread as he sat up.

"I semi-moved out last week," I said quickly, doing my best to take back control of the conversation, before Carlisle could elaborate further. I needed to turn the volume down on my stereo as they both yelled *what?!* on their ends of the line. "Let me explain. Do you both have a bit?" They hummed their agreement and I went on to tell them what all had happened the past week.

As I was getting off the ferry, Wes was the first to say something. *"Wait. You got to hang out with Charlotte yesterday?"* Of course that was his first take away.

"Yes, Wes, and if you were to call her, you could hang out with her, too. It's not my fault she and Desiree drunkenly came home with Ingrid after brunch."

"Wait, so you're living with this girl that you met last week?" Carlisle, the reasonable one, asked.

"Yes, and before you panic, I know this is crazy and insane. I may be able to bring her to the Astor Christmas party this weekend and you two can meet her then."

"You're going to let her meet your mom?" Wes questioned, sounding unsure. I understood his concern with that, but if everything went as planned, they needed to meet sooner than later.

"Considering I'm hoping to propose to her at the end of these three months, I probably should, don't you think?" I answered his question with a question.

"Why do you feel like you need to propose to her this early on though? Why are you living with her?" Carlisle chimed in, adding his own questions to the mix.

"Carlisle, you know dad is ready to pass the company over to me. He won't do that unless I marry. Plus if I take my time, mom is just going to keep trying to throw potential brides at me," I told them. "Look, I know this seems rushed, because it is, but if I didn't genuinely believe that Ingrid might truly be it for me, I wouldn't have done any of this. When you meet her, you'll both understand."

They seemed to accept that answer for the time being. As I pulled into the parking garage, we disconnected our call. Walking into the office, I sent off a text to Ingrid. Of course I would start a relationship with a girl two weeks before the holidays.

> Good morning, little minx. I hope you slept well and had only the filthiest dreams of me. Let me know when you wake up so I can give you a call. We need to talk about the holidays x

I dropped my phone into my pocket as I strode into my office to gather what I needed for the first meeting of the day.

Eleven

Ingrid

When I woke up, I was greeted by a note, cash, and a text message.

Good lord, Josh, what has gotten into you today?

I read his note first and laughed to myself as I snuck the cash into one of his suit pockets in the closet. I could buy my own breakfast. I plopped back down into bed as I pulled my phone off the charger and read over his text.

Most Ineligible Boyfriend in NY

> Good morning, little minx. I hope you slept well and had only the filthiest dreams of me. Let me know when you wake up so I can give you a call. We need to talk about the holidays x

What the hell?

> Good morning, I'm awake now. Also, nice new contact name lol

Quickly changing his name to something much shorter, I saw him typing out his response back.

Joshua Astor (x3)

> What? Last I checked, I'm no longer eligible. Go ahead and get your coffee started, I'll call you in 5

Rolling back out of bed, I walked to my kitchen to do exactly that, making sure to grab my favorite mug along with my lavender syrup.

Hmm, maybe I should get him his own mug now that he's here, I mused as I ground the coffee beans.

Mine was decorated in postage stamps from around the world, glazed with beautiful vibrant colors. I was almost certain I could find one with records covering it for him. I made a mental note for when I went Christmas shopping later that day.

Five minutes went by and sure enough, "Joshua Astor (x3)" popped up on my lock screen. Answering quickly, I put the phone between my shoulder and my ear as I stirred my latte on the way to the couch.

"Alright, coffee is ready and I'm getting comfy on the couch. You said we needed to talk about the holidays?" I asked as I smushed down into the sofa, careful not to spill.

"We do. I was thinking you could join me at my family's annual Christmas party this weekend." I could hear the nerves in his voice as he spoke. Meeting the family was a big deal, but I understood why it was something we needed to do.

"I would love to. I was already planning on reaching out to my dad to let him know I'd be bringing another person next week," I said. "I'm going shopping later today. Can you send me some standard ideas for your parents so I can grab their gifts as well?"

"Wait, you don't have any concerns or anything?" He asked, still seeming nervous.

"No, I figured we should get the family introductions out of the way soon, and what better way than at Christmas?"

"Well," he started and I could feel the tension in his shoulders through the phone, *"my best friends, Carlisle and Wes, will also be there."*

"The more the merrier; however, you're in charge of gifts for your boys. I'll handle the parents, but you know your friends best."

"Alright, sounds good. There's a dress code for the party, just semi-formal. Think office holiday party, just my mom is HR."

"I can work with that, I assume a lot of this is going to be spent networking and shop talk for you?"

"Yeah, that's usually how it goes. With you there with me, it may turn the tides a little."

"I'll be wherever you need me to be. I'm sure some women will want to talk fashion, so don't feel like you can't leave me to my own devices if needed." With him being so clearly nervous about it all, I wanted to be sure I could do whatever he needed to make it easier for him. "Are we mentioning our arrangement at all?"

"I don't think we should," he answered with ease. *"I let the guys know, but I think we should leave both of our parents out of it for now. Just let them see us. The rest will come naturally."*

We wrapped up our conversation as he had another meeting he needed to get to, so I went ahead and got ready for the day. I didn't have any appointments until later in the week, so outside of my shipping, all that was scheduled was working on more sketches for spring. I needed to get those done by mid January so that I could have the dresses made and ready to go for launch in May. I made five dresses for each season, every year. That way I could still put most of my focus on customs.

After taking a quick shower, I threw on a black turtleneck, leggings, my cream fuzzy socks, and tennis shoes. Grabbing my lilac beanie and coat at the last second, I made my way out the door to get started with my day. One of the reasons that I picked the street I did was because of the other businesses that lined it. From chic boutiques, an antique store, my favorite coffee shop, and the pottery shop where I got all of my dishes, I couldn't think of a better spot.

I headed over to *Spill the Beans* across the street first to grab myself a bite to eat and another lavender latte before I popped over to *Ceramix*. I easily found the mug I knew they would have for Josh within just a few minutes of walking in. I loved this store because everything they made was quirky and fun. One of my plates at home was made to look just like a lettuce head. The mug I found for Josh was equally as perfect, not just because of the mini vinyl records spotted on the outside, but they also made the bottom of the well have a record there.

Maybe when we moved, I could have a spot for just our mugs so that they could be displayed next to the coffee bar.

When we move.

We really needed to sit down and look for a place together, but with the holidays approaching and our schedules, it would need to wait a little bit. One thing I knew, I didn't want to be far from my shop, so maybe we would be able to find something where I could either relocate *Love at the Seam*, or the commute would be bearable. I was sure he was wanting to be closer to the office, and would likely need to be once he became the CEO. I couldn't let myself worry about it yet. We needed to make it through the first three months before we discussed it fully. For all we knew, we would be sick of each other by then and moving would just consist of him grabbing his eight boxes worth of belongings back to his own apartment.

Throughout my shopping, I was able to find everything else just as easily. I grabbed an antique cigar humidor for Josh's dad and a gorgeous plum bag for his mom. I made my dad a silk tie every year and planned to do the same for Josh's. He mentioned he was wanting to get my dad something on his own, likely just a bottle of brandy, so that it didn't seem like he went to Christmas empty handed. I told him he didn't need to, but once he had his mind set on something, clearly there was no changing it.

The girls were also easy to shop for. I grabbed new gardening gloves for Char and a new pair of wire cutters for Desi. We always got one another practical gifts, to remind each other how much we admire the work they do. Did it also enable our workaholic tendencies? Probably, but we tried not to think about it too hard.

After getting all of my shopping done, I headed back over to my shop so that I could leave the gifts in the closet down stairs. Something else that I loved about the shops in my area was that they would gift wrap everything for you, so all I needed to do was hide them.

Before I left, I made a quick stop over to the formal dresses I had toward the back of the store. I always kept a few designs on hand that weren't necessarily for weddings just in case anybody needed something last minute. It came in handy, too, because what better way to show up to the Christmas party than in my own gown? Flipping through, I managed to find the burgundy cowl neck slip dress that I was looking for. I had a black coat and simple black heels I could pair with it, upstairs. I giggled to myself as I thought about Josh's reaction, knowing he would lose his mind once he saw it.

Once I was done, I went back upstairs to get going on my work for the rest of the day.

Twelve

Joshua

"Ingrid, sweet girl, are you almost ready?" We were about to head to my parents' annual Christmas party, but a certain little minx had been in the bathroom primping for what seemed like forever. "Get your sexy ass out here, please!"

Listening for once, I heard the door open and the sound of her heels clacking on the floorboards. Walking into the living room, Ingrid was wearing a beautiful deep red dress that looked as if it was made for her skin. She had decided on gold jewelry with emerald stones and her hair was in some kind of updo with pieces loose to frame her face. There was a slit that rode up to her mid-thigh on her left leg. Trailing my eyes down, I saw the simple black heels that made her legs look like they could go on for days, despite knowing how short she really was. I took my time dragging my eyes across every expanse of her as she put in an earring. I watched, with what was probably a predatory gaze, as she walked toward the door, grabbing her long, black coat, before moving to open it. In a flash, I was behind her, trapping her between myself and the wood. She always smelled like lavender and espresso, from the million and one lattes she drank throughout her days, and I breathed her in as I brought my mouth from her neck to her ear.

"You better not be wearing any panties, little minx," I warned as my hand dragged up her left thigh. Bringing my fingers under the slit in her dress, my fingers skimmed across a thin, silky barrier between me and her. "And what, pray tell, is this?" I asked as I pinched the fabric between my fingertips.

"I am *not* ruining the fabric of this dress because you, Joshua Astor the Third, can't keep your hands to yourself the night I meet your family." She sounded confident in her reasoning, but I could tell from the blush spreading across her chest and up her neck that this was exactly what she was hoping to happen. She cleared her throat and brushed my hand to the side so that she could unlock the door. "Come on, Mr. Doesn't Want to be Late. I need to stop downstairs to grab your parents gifts before we go. Can you get the car warmed up please?"

I let her win for the moment, watching as she put her coat on and walked downstairs. Doing as she asked, I left her to get the gifts from her shop while I warmed up the car out front. I watched as she brought back three gifts and methodically locked the store before striding back toward me. Wanting to help her, I got out of the car and met her at the passenger side, opening the door for her and taking the gifts from her hand to place in the trunk. Once I was back in the driver's seat, we made our way toward the ferry.

Out of the corner of my eye, I saw her tugging on her fingers as she looked absentmindedly out of the car window. Hoping to soothe her, I grabbed her hand and brought it to my lips as I asked, "Are you nervous?"

She looked over at me then and I could see her chewing on her lower lip, eyes wide. It took her a moment, but she eventually responded, "Aren't you?"

I considered it for a moment. I'm not nervous about the guys' reactions, I knew they would love her. I was pretty sure my dad would see how happy I was and accept her immediately. My mother on the other hand, I wasn't too sure about. She didn't pick Ingrid, so maybe she would have an issue. The more I thought about it, the more nervous I started to get about everything. Mom only set me up with women of the "housewife" variety, all tall, thin, blonde and spent their hours shopping and whatever else it was they did with a man's money. None of them had anything of substance. None of them had their own dreams that they aspired to or hobbies worth mentioning. Ingrid, on the other hand, was a successful business woman and had managed to make a name for herself outside of her father.

I felt her gaze on me while I thought about everything. Her nerves radiated off of her and seemed to grow the longer I remained quiet.

"No, little minx, I'm not worried. I think they're going to love you," I said in an attempt to calm her some. I couldn't have her breaking down, that would only cause her to feel more uncomfortable all night. I gave her hand another kiss before resting both of ours back on her thigh.

Once we were parked on the ferry, I unbuckled our seatbelts and dragged her over the center console until she was straddling me.

"You didn't seriously believe I was really going to let you win back there, did you?" I shrugged her coat off of her and draped it over the steering wheel at her back. Using the side controls, I moved my seat as far back as it would go to give her a little room right before my hands started inching her dress around her hips. She wasn't wearing a bra and with the neckline of her dress, I was able to easily scoop her breasts out from the top, allowing me access to take one of her perfect nipples into my mouth. I tugged with my teeth before releasing so I could look back at her. "There is only one rule in our house, and that is what, little minx?"

Her hands were on my shoulders as my own stayed tight on her hips. I didn't move to touch her any further, even with her on display for me, both nipples begging for attention.

She squirmed a little before giving in. "No panties."

"That's right, Ingrid. You broke that rule, didn't you?" Reaching behind her, I took my keys out of the ignition and opened the small keychain knife I had dangling there behind her back. I moved gently before slicing through the fabric on both sides of her hips. She let out a harsh gasp as she watched me tug the front of the silk panties from underneath her before I put them in the pocket of my pants.

"Now, that's better, isn't it?" I asked her as I brought my middle finger through her slit before finding her clit. "And look at this, ready for me already." Taking her clit between two of knuckles, I marveled at how responsive she was as I tugged. With all of the work and chaos I knew that brewed in the pretty head of hers, it was incredible to see her give herself to me so easily and let me take control.

We didn't have much time and given her insolence, I didn't want to fuck her just yet. Instead, I used my finger to draw lazy figure eights from her clit to her entrance before shoving it deep inside of her. After one pump, *okay, fine, two*, I removed it from her warmth and brought it up to her lips.

"Open," I demanded. "Now, suck."

She did without hesitation, her plump glossed lips wrapped tightly around my finger as I felt her tongue lick up every drop of her arousal from me. Because I couldn't help myself, when she was done, I moved the same hand to grab her by the throat and pulled her mouth to mine, my tongue instantly claiming ownership.

Groaning, I placed my hands back on her hips before lifting her and dropping her back into her own seat. The ferry would be docking soon which meant, as much as it pained me, we would have to wait to continue. I handed her back her coat as I moved my seat back into its position and started up the car. Once I knew we were both buckled safely, I started the drive to my parents.

Under her breath, I heard her calling me an insufferable ass. I didn't even bother stifling my laughter as I grabbed her hand.

"Joshua, oh come here! You haven't returned any of my calls, I wasn't sure if you were even coming this evening!" My mother dragged me into a hug before it could be stopped. I was forced to let go of Ingrid's hand and pass the gifts off to her so I wouldn't drop them.

"Hey mom. I know, I'm sorry." I moved to break the hug before adding, "I need you to let go of me, though. I have somebody for you to meet." She dropped her arms instantly and attempted to peer around me. I bellowed for my dad to come over from where he was. Once he was by mom's side, I stepped over.

"Mom, dad, I'd like you both to meet my girlfriend, Ingrid." Ingrid was in the middle of taking her coat off while trying to balance the gifts and maneuver at the same time. Chuckling, I grabbed the gifts from her before she threw them in frustration. "Sorry, love."

She gave me a soft smile as she got herself together and then turned to my parents. "Hi, it's so nice to meet you both! I hope it's alright that I join this evening, I know how much planning goes into guest lists and I truly don't mean to be a party crasher." She reached her hand out to shake both of theirs. My dad's smile gleamed from ear to ear as he took in my little chaos storm. He was the first to shake her hand.

"It's lovely to meet you, Ingrid. As I'm sure you know, I'm Josh Jr and this is my wife Quinn," he said, nodding his head in the direction of mom. I looked at mom then, only to see her dragging her eyes up and down the length of Ingrid. I noted a hint of annoyance in her gaze before she quickly masked it.

"Let's move out of the foyer and go have a seat in the drawing room. The rest of the guests aren't here yet," she said as she turned on her heel, making the three of us follow after her. *Lovely*. Once we were all seated, mom wasted no time beginning her line of questioning.

"Tell me, how did you two meet?" she asked, almost sounding like she didn't believe our relationship was true.

"I helped Wes with a wedding expo last week," I explained. "Ingrid was running her own booth. You may be familiar with her designs, mom. She owns *Love at the Seam*." I would always take every opportunity to brag about what an amazing woman she was. "She was recently featured in a wedding magazine!"

Mom tilted her head at this and almost looked surprised. Dad, again, was the first to respond. "So you're a wedding dress designer?"

Ingrid nodded. "I am! My boutique is in Staten Island and I've been in the business for the past three years or so. The wedding expos are honestly what's helped raise it off the ground." The pride in her eyes and tone was clear as she talked about her work. She should be proud, her talent was immeasurable.

I could see the wheels spinning in my moms head as she tried to determine just how to test my girl. Eventually, she decided the direction she wanted to go and narrowed her eyes. "Being in the wedding business, I'm sure you jumped at the chance to be with one of New York's most eligible bachelors." She was zoned in on Ingrid, never wavering and as much as I wanted to step in, I knew Ingrid could handle her own and would want to. "He's been a topic of conversation amongst women in this city since the article came out, you know." Ingrid and I both shared a laugh. We both knew the article wasn't why she gave me her number.

"Given that I make custom gowns, I really only speak with my brides about what their dress visions are," Ingrid said with a hint of amusement in her tone. "I don't pay attention to local celebrity gossip, seeing as I've dealt with it my entire life. You know, being Senator Morgan's daughter and all." I pressed my fist to my mouth and coughed to try hiding the laugh that escaped as she went on. "It's funny, I actually didn't even know about that article until *after* I met him. Shamelessly, I did buy a copy and have it on my bookshelf next to the wedding magazine that I'm featured in."

That's my girl.

It was interesting to see my mother stunned. She couldn't figure out how to respond to her and my father took over the reins with ease. "Senator Morgan! I knew you looked familiar but couldn't quite place it. Good man, your father. Rest assured, he got my vote." He turned to me and asked, "Have you met him yet, son?"

"Not yet. I'm going with her to her dad's for Christmas with her friends next week, so I'll meet him then." He nodded his approval while mom continued gawking as she tried to figure out what her next move was.

"Well, let's go ahead and get the family presents out of the way before the party starts," she said, dismissing all previous talk from the room. She looked at Ingrid with mock pity. "I do apologize, we didn't get you anything seeing as we didn't know you were coming."

"Oh that's more than alright," Ingrid waved her off. "The act of gift giving is my favorite part of the holidays. I'm just grateful that you both are alright with me joining." She was playing the game my mother dealt well. I knew she wanted to win my mom over and I only hoped that mom would respect her more if Ingrid was able to bite back with the same grace.

I passed my parents their gifts and we opened them together. Ingrid and I were waiting until the following week for our own exchange, so she watched nervously as my parents opened their gifts. She managed to find a gorgeous antique cigar humidor for my father along with sewing him an exquisite midnight blue tie. She told him how she made one for her dad every year for Christmas and wanted to include him in the tradition. He absolutely beamed as he admired her work and complimented the fabric and stitching. I let her know some basic information about my parents before she went on her shopping trip the other day, so I knew mom should love the plum purse that she was now holding, seeing as it was her favorite color. She studied it for a moment before she eventually thanked Ingrid for the gift. It became increasingly more clear that my mother wouldn't be making it easy for Ingrid to come into the family.

The ladies eventually left the room as guests started to arrive and my dad asked that I stay back.

"Give her time. She'll come around," he said as he passed me my gift, a cigar. He gave one to Wes, Carlisle, and myself every year. "You light up around her. Is this where you've been the past couple of weeks? With her?" Don't think I haven't noticed that you've been working from home more." My dad and I have always been close, so I knew lying to him would be futile. I decided to be honest with him as we started walking toward his study. I could hear the guys behind us talking to each other as they followed, seeming to have just arrived at the party.

Might as well have this conversation with them here to back me up, I thought to myself as I followed my dad to his study.

I waited until we were all seated with cigars lit. When the room started to slowly fill with clouds of smoke, I told him everything.

"I'm not going to lecture you about this, son," he said as he puffed on his cigar. "I've always admired how you're never afraid to go after what you want, no matter the route that you need to take to do so. She makes you happy, I can see that clear as day when you're with her and when you talk about her." I forced my jaw to not drop as I sat stunned by his words.

I cleared my throat. "I ask that you don't tell mom about mine and Ingrid's arrangement. I don't want her to think this is just to get her off my back." It was bad enough that she was giving Ingrid a hard time, I didn't want to make matters worse.

"Your secret is safe with me," he promised with a nod of his head. "You might not want her father to know about it either, but trust her judgement if she chooses to tell him."

Suddenly, Carlisle clapped his hands and rubbed them together, getting to his feet in excitement. "Alright, is it my turn to finally meet her?" We all laughed as we left the study to join the party in search of my girl.

Thirteen

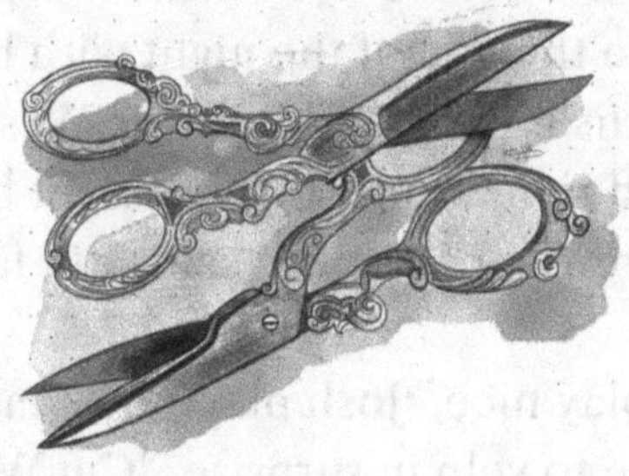

Ingrid

I followed behind Quinn as she walked me out to the main living room where the party was being held. Guests had begun arriving while we were in the drawing room and I took in my surroundings a little more as I heard them mingling around us. His parents truly had a lovely home. Don't get me wrong, it was an absolute mansion, but there were touches of personality sprinkled in with the elaborate decor and I could tell love lived there. Quinn pointed out the open bar as she excused herself to go play hostess with her guests.

Ordering myself an espresso martini, I felt hands creep up around my sides as Josh ordered himself a bourbon old fashioned. I breathed in his tobacco and vanilla scent as he brought his mouth to my ear and whispered, "Ready to meet my friends?"

I nodded excitedly as we grabbed our drinks, thanked the bartender, and turned so he could introduce me to Wesley and Carlisle, both of them giving me welcoming smiles.

"Hey Wes, have you called her yet?" I asked in way of a greeting. Josh may have said that he didn't want to get involved, but I knew he had her business card in his pocket to give him before the end of the night with her cell number on the back. Carlisle laughed loudly as Wes's smile turned into a glare aimed right at me. I glared right back.

"Okay, you were right," Carlisle said, still laughing. "I love her already."

"Now, Ingrid, play nice," Josh playfully chastised, swatting my ass causing me to yelp in surprise. "Cut Wes a break, he's shy."

"Carlisle, it's great to finally meet you," I told him as I shook his hand before turning back toward Wes. "It's good to see you again from outside your booth." He smiled hesitantly as he shook my hand.

"I'm going to call her, I promise," he vowed and I could see the determination in his eyes. Maybe he just needed one of her friends to give him the push. Not subtly in the slightest, I nudged Josh with my elbow to get him to give the card over. He humored me and when Wes flipped it over and saw Char's number there plain as day, his eyes lit up and his thumb swiped over it once before he pocketed the card.

"What? No gift for me this year?" Carlisle pouted at us. Josh rolled his eyes and handed him over a full flask of single malt scotch. Carlisle hugged it to his chest. "For me? You shouldn't have." We all laughed as he proceeded to flick open the flask and down a shot's worth.

The men continued with their gift exchanges, giving Josh their gifts to him. Wes had gotten him a gift card to a record store and

Carlisle had given him a new keychain knife. Josh chuckled at it as Carlisle said, "I figured your current one was getting dull."

Oh, how wrong he was.

The party continued on with Josh keeping me on his arm, proudly introducing me to anybody that would listen. I spotted Quinn off to the side, seeming to take a short break away from the excitement and I excused myself to go speak with her.

"The party is beautiful, Quinn," I said as I approached her side.

"It's Mrs. Astor," she hissed. I didn't look in her direction, which she clearly hoped for as her glare burned into my profile, I just simply watched the party happening in front of us while she stewed. "Do you honestly think this little fling with my son is going to turn into something more?"

Catching sight of her son in question, his head was tilted back in a laugh as Carlisle had passed the flask to Wes who seemed to be coughing from the burn of the scotch. I smiled in their direction before turning to face her, ensuring my features remained calm and relaxed. "I hope so. I've never felt the kind of happiness that he's given me since entering my life. If I'm able to give him even an ounce of the same level of joy, then I truly hope that he finds it in him to keep me around." I turned my attention back over to the boys, who were still laughing loudly with one another. I couldn't stop the smile that spread on my face if I tried.

"Surely you know that to join this family, you'd need to shut your business down to tend to the home," she said cooly in an attempt to discourage me. "He needs a wife that will plan his events and watch after the children. Your mother must have failed in teaching you these things."

Taking slow, calculating breaths, I refrained from my knee jerk reaction of slapping the shit out of her, but not before a gasp escaped my lips. As I turned my body to face her completely,

I caught movement of somebody approaching us out of the corner of my eye. Paying them no mind, and leveling her with a look, I said, "Considering my mother has been dead since I was born, I guess you're right in that she didn't get to teach me how to be a housewife." I tried not to take satisfaction out of the way her eyes doubled in size at the information, but I couldn't help it.

Good, I thought to myself, *serves you right.*

I didn't give her a chance to respond as I continued on. "In case you've forgotten, I work in the wedding industry, meaning I know more event planners than I could even dream of needing. The great part about my job is that I get to spend a lot of my time in the comfort of my home as I don't need to leave to draw sketches. I don't know why you believe that women can't be both successful on their own as well as amazing wives and mothers, but I assure you it's very possible. I hope you're able to look past this enough one day to let me in."

As I turned on my heel to walk away, I noticed Josh was barely two feet behind me. I could see the anger rolling off of him in waves, crashing into and mixing with the hurt swiping in his eyes as he glared right at his mother. He grabbed my wrist as I made to move past him and pulled me into his side.

"Merry Christmas, mother." I couldn't see her but I heard her small scoff at the name change. He didn't allow her to respond as he said, "Give my love to dad. Ingrid and I are leaving." He didn't spare her another glance as he turned us both to walk toward the door. I heard her calling out his name behind us, but he just kept walking.

I did my best to keep my breaths even as I willed myself not to cry. My hands were shaking as he draped my coat over my shoulders. Josh noticed my tremble and pulled them into his own, squeezing tight. He seemed like he was about to say something, but Carlisle and Wes appeared next to us before he could.

"If you two are leaving, so are we," Carlisle said with a shrug of his shoulders.

"How about we all go to the penthouse?" Wes suggested. He looked over at me and asked, "Have you seen it yet, Ingrid?"

I shook my head no and looked up at Josh who was silently asking if it would be alright. I thought a distraction would do us both some good and I wanted to get to know his friends more. I gave him a small nod of approval and he looked up at the guys to say, "That works. Meet us there."

We sat in uncomfortable silence during the car ride. Unable to take it any longer, I finally burst the bubble and turned to look at him, tugging on my fingers and said, "I'm sorry for snapping at her."

We were stopped at a red light so he took the opportunity to look over at me. His expression appeared almost puzzled as he asked, "Why the fuck are you apologizing? She had that coming after what she said to you." As his words registered, I let out a sigh of relief as I realized he wasn't upset with me.

"Let's not talk about this anymore then. I don't want to get between you and your mom. I really do hope she will let me in and allow a relationship to grow between us one day," I said, making sure to hold his gaze, only breaking it when the light turned green to allow him to face the road once more. As he turned into the parking garage, I continued, "It'll be okay. I'm still here and I'm not going anywhere. She can't be upset with you forever. Now, let's go hang out with your friends. Are we staying here tonight?"

He parked the car and opened the passenger door for me, keeping his hand on the small of my back as he led us toward the elevator. "If it's alright with you, I'd like that. I'm sure I have something comfortable you can wear tomorrow so that you don't need to stay in your dress."

We were still waiting for the elevator to come down as the guys pulled into the parking garage. As they walked toward us, the doors opened and we held them while Wes and Carlisle jogged inside. The three of them joked around as we were lifted up, up, *up*, toward the penthouse. Once we made it to the top floor, I realized the elevator was essentially his front door as it opened directly inside for him. He must have used a key or something on the elevator that I missed while the guys were getting on.

Hand back at the small of my back, he led me through the corridor and I took everything in as we ventured further inside. The first thing I noticed was that it smelled like him, traces of tobacco and vanilla lingered throughout the space despite his lack of being there recently. He also had a more rustic design choice than what I imagined him having. Dark, aged wood tones were scattered throughout mixed with warm colors of mustard yellow and burnt orange. As I continued to observe, I noticed our tastes weren't much different from each other. One wall in the living room had floor to ceiling shelves covered in his vinyl collection, the stereo system missing from its obvious spot in the center. I laughed to myself as I thought about it sitting next to my books back at my place. Now that I could see the amount of belongings he had, I was struck again that we would need to figure out our living situation at some point. I tried to brush it off for the time being as I plopped down onto his sectional sofa.

Dammit, it's comfier than mine.

"You hungry, little minx?" Josh called out to me from the kitchen. I nodded eagerly. I hadn't eaten at his parents house, too consumed with nervous energy and was famished to say the least. Josh opened his fridge and I heard him laugh as he said, "Oh right, I moved out. There's no food here."

"Pizza?" Wes asked as he made his way over to the couch. He found a beer from somewhere, so I could only assume Josh left those behind.

"Works for me!" Carlisle announced as he jumped over the back of the couch and landed next to Wes, also with a beer in hand. I twisted around to look for Josh and saw him walking over, carrying two beers.

Leaning over the back of the couch to kiss me on the cheek, he whispered in my ear, "After pizza, I will be kicking them out. Don't think I've forgotten about our little game that we were playing earlier." He handed me a beer and I tried to play it off like the cold glass was the reason for my shiver, though I knew I wasn't fooling anybody if the heat I felt creeping up my cheeks was anything to go by. The moment Josh sat down next to me, I stood before he could pull me into him. "Little minx?" He asked, looking up at me confused as he tried to figure out what I was up to.

"I'm not eating pizza in this dress. This took me ten hours to sew. Which door is your room?" Oh, I was in for it if the look he was giving me was anything to go by. I could tell he was disappointed that he wouldn't be the one to remove my dress, but oh well. He eyed me carefully as he took a sip from his beer before pointing with the spout toward the door down the hall.

"T-shirts are in the middle drawer with my sweats in the bottom," he said, still eyeing me. "Pepperoni on your pizza, right?" I nodded approvingly and walked toward the bedroom. I could hear the guys giving him shit as I walked in and shut the door. I couldn't help but laugh to myself as I walked toward his closet, spotting his dresser in there.

Quickly, I put on one of his seemingly more worn t-shirts, a simple one from a music festival years ago. I pulled out sweat pants from his bottom drawer but before I put them on, an idea crossed my brain. Opening up the top drawer, I found his socks and boxers. Without allowing myself to second guess the choice I was about to make, I grabbed a black pair of briefs and put them on before gliding into the sweat pants and partially tucking the hem of the tee into the waistband. I needed to tighten the drawstrings as far as they would go and roll the hem over a couple of times to keep them from falling, but once I had them sorted, I felt presentable enough clothes wise.

Once I was dressed, I carefully placed my jewelry on top of the dresser and then went into his en suite bathroom to find some form of face wash. Luckily, he had a few products that he didn't move with so I was able to do a light skin care routine. I left my hair be, since I had really just thrown it into a pretty, yet messy, bun.

"Hey little minx, pizza will be here in twenty," Josh said from his spot on the couch.

As I took my seat next to him, I finally opened my beer and took a sip, grateful that it was still cold. Carlisle and Wes were sitting up and watching me as they waited for me to put it back down.

Ah, my turn it is then.

"So, what are your intentions with our best friend?" Carlisle asked, trying to force any trace of amusement off of his face.

"Clearly, I'm here to marry rich and widow richer," I deadpanned. Wes couldn't help the laugh from escaping, choking on the sip he'd taken, and I could feel Josh pinch my side. I held Carlisle's stare as I then said, "I have no intentions outside of the arrangement you're already aware of. If you have questions for why the arrangement exists to begin with, you'll need to talk to him. All I did was hear him out and take the leap he asked me for."

"Well then, I hope you understand that if you break his heart that also means you'll break Wes's because then he'll never get the nerve to call your florist friend," Carlisle jokes. I looked over at Wes then, seeing him wincing a little.

"Ah, so that's why you aren't interrogating me. You're worried that I'll turn the line of questioning back to you," I said, narrowing my eyes at him. "You have her number, just send her a text. She isn't going to wait forever. But hear me when I tell you, she's been pining for you since the first expo you showed up at. If you break her heart, I have fabric scissors with your name on them."

"What is it with you and Charlotte's need to threaten with sharp objects? First gardening shears and now this?" Josh asked as his hand teased under the hem of his shirt I was wearing. His fingers drew small circles on my skin at my side and I leaned into him further as I shrugged.

"I'm shocked Desi didn't threaten you with the wire cutters, if I'm being honest. Although, you did babysit our drunk asses and then fed us, so you're likely on her good list for now."

"Desi?" Carlisle asked.

"Yeah, she's my other best friend, Desiree. She owns her own jewelry store, *Estelle Jewels*. The three of us met at a wedding expo a few years ago and have been inseparable ever since."

"Interesting. Stay away from the crazy lady with the wire cutters, the other crazy lady with the gardening shears, and now this crazy lady with the fabric scissors. Got it." He laughed a little and then looked over to Josh to jump into a conversation about work.

Wes and I moved into casual conversation about the brides we both had and he showed me some of the designs he was working on for our shared *Lord of the Rings* couple. When

Carlisle eventually got up to grab the pizza, I saw Wes staring at his screen intently. I left him to that while I felt Josh's hand snake to the waistband of the sweats. Pushing his fingers just under the top of the fabric, his hand stilled as he felt the briefs. I hid my chuckle as I looked up at him, only to find him squinting at me.

Before Carlisle reached us, I leaned up a little to whisper, "What? You said no panties. You said nothing about wearing boxers." Leaving him to growl in frustration, I sat up and patted him on the thigh as Carlisle placed the pizza boxes onto the coffee table.

Once we all finished eating, Josh stood up before leaning down to throw me over his shoulder. "Alright you two, get out so I can fuck my future wife." I swatted at him and yelled his name as I heard the guys laugh and quickly exit the penthouse on our way to the bedroom.

Fourteen

Joshua

I swore, this woman was going to be the absolute death of me. Carrying her into my room, I threw her down onto the mattress and watched as her whole body bounced. I looked down at her to see a grin on her face like she just *knew* she was in trouble and couldn't be more pleased with herself. Unbuttoning my shirt and peeling it off, I watched her hazel eyes travel down the length of my chest and torso. She made a move to take off the shirt she was wearing to follow my lead, but I leant down to slap her hand away before she could.

"Absolutely not," I scolded her. "First the panties, then I didn't get to be the one to take that dress off of you, and now my boxers?" Don't get me wrong, her being in my clothes in general was hot, but she was testing me and she knew it. "It's my turn, now."

I undid my belt buckle, yanked my belt out of the loops, and pulled my pants off while leaving on my briefs, my cock straining with discomfort more than it had all evening. I hadn't had a clear head since the moment she walked out of the bathroom before we left. She was back in her kneeling position at the edge of the bed and as I walked toward her, she backed up a little bit. I bent down just a touch and watched her reaction as I placed the belt on the bed next to her.

"Stand." She listened with a hint of hesitation, not knowing what I was planning. Once she was right in front of me, I tapped the sides of her arms and ordered, "Up." Once her arms were in the air, I lifted my shirt off of her before tossing it to the floor. Getting on my knees, I traced my mouth over her skin, not giving her the direct attention she was aching for. I took my time unrolling the waistband of the sweats and tugged the drawstrings undone with my teeth, causing the sweats to drop off of her at once. I slapped her hands away again, and gave her a pointed look when she tried to pull the briefs down before doing it myself and letting her step out of them.

Tapping the inside of her ankles with one hand, I said, "Wider." This time, there was no trace of hesitation as she immediately fixed her stance, allowing me access to what I was wanting. I traced the same fingers up the inside of her leg before I dragged my middle finger through her slit.

"Still so wet for me this evening. Tell me, has it been this bad since the ferry?" I traced circles around her clit without giving it any direct attention while she moved to grab my hair. I swatted her away again, glad for the plan I had worked up, and said, "I asked you a question, little minx. Might be in your best interest to answer me."

As I brought my finger down to her entrance then back up to trace around her clit, teasing her further, she moaned. "Yes. Josh, please."

"Oh no, you aren't getting off that easy tonight," I told her before dropping my hand and moving to stand. I licked my finger clean, just needing to taste her. "Get on your knees and face the headboard."

I watched as she did as I asked, crawling her way up the mattress and into position for me. I had her scoot back just enough to hold her wrists out in front of her. Grabbing the belt from the bed, I quickly bound her wrists and then attached it to the top of the metal headboard. Her eyes followed me as much as she could as I walked back over to where my pants were discarded on the floor and reached into the pocket to grab her cut panties from the ferry. Once I was back at her side, I tapped on her chin to silently request she open up her mouth. Her eyes sparkled with excitement as she opened wide enough for me to stuff her panties inside.

As I moved into position behind her, lifting her hips so that she was at the angle I needed, I grabbed her by her hair and turned her so I could make some eye contact with her. "If at any point you want me to let you down or stop, tap me with your foot twice," I instructed. "Do it now to let me know you understand." I waited to let go of her until I felt the tap of her foot on my leg.

With her permission given, I released her and planted a kiss between her shoulder blades while I trailed my hand around her side until my fingers were back where we both wanted them. Feeling her arch further beneath my touch, I began playing with her clit, just to give her some of the stimulation she was craving. I removed my hand again and traced her spine with my tongue as I moved further down her body. A muffled yelp and moan escaped her as I bit her ass cheek and then licked up her center.

"You're being such a good girl now that I have you tied up," I crooned. "I'll have to remember this for the next time you decide to be a brat."

I continued my movements, taunting her as I licked from entrance to clit and back again. She tasted so fucking good, I had to stop myself from just burying my tongue deep inside her tight cunt. I was going to give into her soon, I could barely contain myself as it was.

Sitting up, I worked my own briefs off and tossed them off the bed. Palming my finally free erection, I cupped her pussy in my other hand. I leaned over and bit her opposite cheek before soothing it with a kiss. Wanting to give her a small reprieve for being good, I slid my thumb into her and curled it while I pinched her clit between my middle and ring fingers. I listened to more of her quiet moans as she relished in the attention. When I removed my hand completely, those moans quickly turned into a grunt of frustration.

"Aw, is my little minx needing more?" I asked her, pretending like I wasn't also desperate for more. I slapped her ass hard enough to see an imprint of my hand before I nestled between her thighs. Slowly, I pushed just the tip of my cock into her. Already, I could feel her trying to squeeze around me as she tried to back further against me to take more.

"Say please and I just might give you what you're wanting," I said as I leaned forward to remove the makeshift gag, careful not to push more inside of her.

"Please, Josh, I need you inside of me," she let out on a breathy moan.

"As you insist." I slowly pushed all the way into her, my arms crossed at my chest to force myself not to grip her hard and pound into her. I could see her looking over her shoulder, confusion consumed her face as I remained still.

"If you're wanting more, take it."

I watched as she began to understand, a determined look in her eye. She wiggled her wrists until she was able to grab ahold of the belt above her and I watched, transfixed, as my little minx used this to help hoist herself higher on my dick. Looking down, I watched as she began to do exactly as I said and fucked herself on my length. She set a steady pace and from the sounds that came out of her, I could tell she was having the time of her life. I could feel her getting close to reaching the orgasm I've kept just out of reach for her all night, so to help, I reached my hand around and pinched her clit one more time, hard.

"Let go for me," I said through gritted teeth. She clenched hard as her orgasm consumed her entire body and I had to grab ahold of her hips to keep myself steady to avoid following her into bliss. I took over and pumped in and out of her at a fast, hard pace, throwing her from one orgasm and into another. Lifting her slightly, I moved us both forward, just enough so that I could grab onto her hair and tug her head back so that she was forced to look up. Right as I was about to come, I wrapped my other arm around her waist and flattened my chest to her back, making sure never to break the punishing rhythm I set. "One more, Ingrid. You can do it." I sucked the lobe of her ear into my mouth, biting it before moving my mouth to suck on the pulse point directly below it. She screamed as she came one last time and I let myself follow her, stars blocking my vision just like they always did when I was with her.

"I love you," I muttered, before I could stop myself. I didn't try to take the words back, I didn't expect for her to respond. I heard a sharp inhale of her breath as I pulled out of her before I reached up to undo the belt. Once her arms were back down, I massaged feeling back into her wrists and slowly realized she hadn't stopped staring at me. I could feel her gaze as I lifted her wrists to my mouth and kissed them softly. When I finally met her eyes, there were tears flicking off of her lashes.

Fuck, was I too rough with her? Did she tap me and I missed it?

Just as I was about to apologize, I heard her softly say, "I love you, too, Josh."

I put her arms around my neck and carried her out of the bed and into my en suite. I placed her on the floor, just long enough for me to turn the shower on before I picked her right back up so that her legs wrapped around my waist. In the walk-in, I pressed her against the wall and kissed her.

This girl. This wonderful, intelligent, successful, brilliant woman. I wasn't worried about what would happen at the end of our arrangement, I already knew I was marrying her. If I had a ring, I would have been proposing to her right then. I knew the moment I first saw her that she was the only woman I would ever want, could ever need. Now that I had her, I was never letting her go.

Breaking our kiss, she looked at me with a smile on her face that made me melt. "Josh, the water is going to get cold."

I leaned back into her neck and said, "I don't give a fuck about the water, my girl loves me."

Fifteen

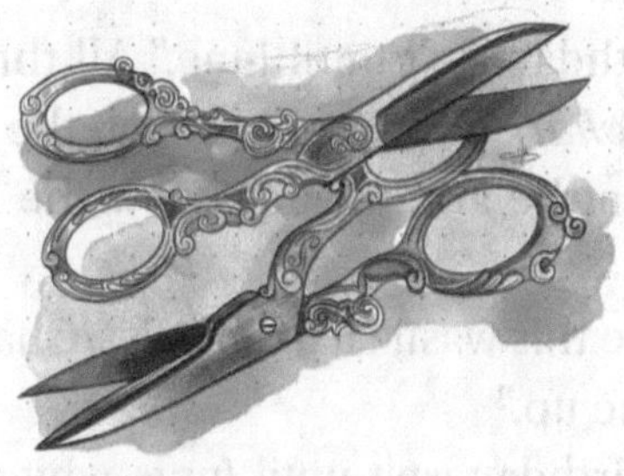

Ingrid

"So, Char, any updates yet?" We were all piled into a rented SUV as we headed to Newburgh for Christmas weekend. I was sitting up front, scrolling through the playlist to pick what to listen to, while the girls sat in the back seat as Josh drove us to my dad's.

"I am *not* talking about this right now," Char glared at me and then looked pointedly at Josh.

"If I tell you a secret, will you tell us the news, Charlotte?" Josh asked from the driver's seat, glancing at her in the review mirror. He liked to pretend he didn't care about the Wes and Char situation, but he wasn't being very convincing and I had to cover my face with my hand in an attempt to hide my amused smile.

"Ooo, what secret?" Desi piped in, setting her phone down in her lap and looked wide eyed between me and him. I shrugged, I wasn't sure what secret he was talking about.

"A Wes secret."

Char huffed but caved like I expected her to. "Fine, but you spill first."

"His mom's birthday isn't until June." All three of us gasped and a chorus of "*what?!*" bounced through the car.

Slapping him on the arm, I said, "How the hell haven't you told me this yet?"

He shrugged like this wasn't a major Wes/Char plot point thus far. "It hadn't come up."

"If his mom's birthday isn't until June, why did he place the order at the expo?" Char asked, tilting her head to the side as she tried to figure it out.

"Because he wanted an excuse to talk to you," Josh said, shrugging again. "Are you going to spill the tea, or what?"

I stared at him in pure shock and needed to remind myself to close my mouth to stop looking like a gaping fish. He *really* wasn't doing a good job of playing indifferent about those two. Which, mind you, was fine by me. I couldn't wait to gossip with him.

"He texted me," she sighed. "I don't even know how he got my number."

"Josh did it!" It was his turn to look shocked and I simply shrugged back at him. "Well, you did."

"I thought you weren't getting involved," Desi teased from behind him. He should've known better than to think we all wouldn't mess with him about this at some point.

"I figured her number would be a good Christmas gift. In case you two have forgotten, I'm hoping to marry this little minx and it would be helpful if one of her bridesmaids and one of my groomsmen didn't avoid each other like the plague on the big day." I watched the girls reaction as he spoke, both of them looked at him like he had three heads and then looked back at me. Slowly, they both smiled in a way that made my heart hurt. Wanting to get back on track, Josh asked, "So, what did he say?"

"He said 'hey, this is Wes from the wedding expo. Is this Charlotte Bayne's number?'"

Oh Wes.

"Well, did you respond?" Desi nudged her.

"I just said, 'Hey Wes, yeah this is Char! Did you have a question about the flowers? Also, how did you get this number?'"

She scrunched her face as she stared down at her phone. "Did he say anything back?" I finally asked.

"No, but now that I know how he got my number, it makes sense, I guess." I watched as she started typing furiously.

Laughing, I said, "Oh, don't give him too hard of a time. He's been working up the courage to reach out to you the past couple of weeks. Maybe *you* could ask *him* out."

"Whatever," she grumbled, and I watched as she started hitting the backspace repeatedly on her keyboard before typing out something different.

"Hey, remember, I need you two to get along!" Josh said, looking at her in the mirror again.

"And what about me? Do I need to get along with Carlisle?" Desi questioned.

Josh and I shared a look, nodding to each other. "Yes," we both said in unison.

Pulling into my father's driveway, Josh took a steady breath. I never actually warned my dad that I would be bringing somebody else with us, let alone admitting to bringing a *man*. I figured it would be a nice surprise seeing how that was what he was wanting to begin with.

"Hey." I placed my hand on Josh's knee. "It's going to be fine. He's going to love you."

The girls got out of the SUV and popped the trunk to gather their overnight bags and presents. Josh was still staring ahead as they made it all the way to the front door, seeming to not realize we were still in the car.

"If he doesn't, will you still love me?" Josh asked, so quietly I almost didn't catch it. He finally turned to look at me and his nerves were etched deep into his face.

Reaching my hand up, I smoothed away the line in his face as I said, "Of course, I will. Now, come on. Let's go before he sees us just sitting here." Leaning up, I gave him a quick kiss before getting out of the car. Josh followed suit and went to the still open trunk to grab what was left.

With Josh still behind the car, dad opened the front door and hugged both of the girls tight before hollering to me, "Don't tell me you finally hired a driver!"

"Not exactly," I laughed. Josh started walking toward me, both of our bags over his shoulder and the gift tote in one of his hands. The girls were already inside, leaving us defenseless and I could have sworn I heard them giggle as they retreated. Dad glanced between them and us, the confusion on his face growing stronger as each second passed. "Dad, I'd like you to meet my boyfriend, Joshua Astor. I'm sorry I didn't warn you beforehand, but I thought you might like the surprise." His eyebrows shot straight up to his hairline as he moved to shake Josh's outstretched hand.

"Boyfriend? Wait, Astor? As in *Astor Investments*?" Dad asked, looking between the two of us.

"The one and only. Well, company that is. I'm technically the third of my name. Currently, I'm the COO." Josh smiled as their shake ended.

"Let us in please, I'm cold and I want to hug you," I told dad, making hand movements to get inside. He muttered an apology like he hadn't even realized we hadn't moved from the front step yet and quickly moved to let us in. I pointed Josh in the direction of the living room so that I could talk to my dad privately for a second.

"Two and a half weeks ago, you said you were going to start going out," dad started, looking in the direction Josh was headed. "Now there's a man in my house other than myself?"

"I know, and as much as I don't necessarily want to tell you how this all happened, I don't think there's going to be any other way to explain it," I winced. Josh and I had agreed after his family's party that it would be good to be honest with my dad, especially since he had been honest with his. "Let me show him where to put our things and then you and I can go talk."

Leaving him stunned, I grabbed Josh's hand in the living room and brought him upstairs to my old room. Once everything was set down, he wrapped me in his arms and I took strength in his warm, tobacco and vanilla scent as I readied myself to have the conversation with my dad. He held my hand the whole way back down the stairs and as I left him with the girls in the living room, I could see the faint hint of worry in his eyes.

Everything would be okay, I thought to myself as I headed straight toward my dad's study.

As I gave him a brief rundown of what had happened in my life since I last saw him, he stayed quiet until I was done. While he listened, I could see that he was fighting between likely wanting to kill Josh and just wanting to be happy for me. He took a moment for the information to sink in once I'd finished before he took a breath and straightened.

"When I first met your mother, I knew without a shadow of a doubt that she was going to be the woman I loved for the rest of my life." I stilled at his words, holding my breath as he talked about a mother I would never have the chance to know. "I know I probably should've tried to remarry, give you some siblings, learn how to love again after her, but I never could. Ellie was my light and my joy and my comfort. If it weren't for you being born, I don't know if I ever would have loved another woman outside of her. I see it, in your eyes. When you talk about him, you resemble her so much. I don't need to ask if you're happy, I can see it all over your face. That's all I have ever wanted for you, this amount of just pure happiness."

I didn't realize I was crying until I felt a tear drop to my hands below my face. "Thank you, dad. I know our situation is a little different, but I've never been so happy in my life."

"Different is good, sometimes." The smile on his face was so warm and full of love. "Now, bring him in here. Sounds to me like somebody needs to ask for my blessing."

When I made it back to the living room, I pulled Josh aside so I could point him in the direction of my dad's study. The moment he saw the tears that had started to dry on my cheeks, he tugged me to a stop and grabbed my face in both hands.

"Ingrid, sweetheart, what's wrong? What happened?" His thumbs were frantically trying to wipe whatever was left away as he scanned my face to try to gauge how the conversation with my dad went.

I gave him a smile and laughed a little as I brushed his hands away. "I'm fine, I promise. Happy tears. Well, mostly, kind of. Doesn't matter. He would like to speak with you. His study is down the hall, second door on the right."

He raised an eyebrow but seemed to accept my ramble of an answer as he pulled me in for a tight hug and planted a kiss on top of my head. "I love you," he whispered before letting me go and walked toward my father with his head high and back straight.

Damn, determined Josh was so hot.

Sixteen

Joshua

Senator Morgan's study was cozier than I initially thought it would be. It was all oak wood and warm leather. It reminded me of the grandfather's study in that show Ingrid always made me watch, but with more personal touches. There were bookshelves covering both side walls that housed beautiful first editions and scattered pictures of his family throughout.

"Come in, boy, let's get this over with." The senator seemed calmer than I was expecting him to be. He was grinning at me like he was fully prepared to make me work for our conversation to go my way. When I sat down in the seat across from his desk, I was hit with the lingering smell of lavender and espresso and the chair was still a little warm, confirming for me Ingrid was just sitting in the same seat. Sinking into it, I immediately felt more confident with the small comfort.

"Before we get started, my dad wanted to make sure that I told you that you have his vote every time you run," I said with a smile. He laughed a little and I could see that same prideful joy in his eyes that I saw in his daughter's anytime she discussed her work.

"I'll be sure to thank him when I meet him." He leaned back in his chair, arms folded casually across his stomach. "Now, I believe you have a question for me." He was right, I did, but when I opened my mouth to ask, he raised one hand and cut me off before I could get the words out.

"Don't ask me yet. I understand you'll be here the whole time the girls are. I can already tell from the way my daughter talks about you that she is in love with you. I don't want to hear you tell me all of the reasons why you decided on this *agreement* you two have, I don't even want to hear you tell me how much you care about her. I want you to *show* me. I'm not going to interrogate you, I'm sure you got enough of that from the girls already. I know your intentions, I just want to see how you are with her. Before you leave the day after tomorrow, ask me on your way out. I'll have my answer by then."

I opened and closed my mouth so many times, I was sure I looked ridiculous. I didn't really know what to say to that considering I was the COO of a world renowned corporation, and the fact that I was stunned speechless was strange, to say the least. Instead of attempting to say anything for fear of it coming out as *huh*, I gave a curt nod of my head

Standing, he said, "Good, let's get out there before those girls burn my house down. They should be in the kitchen by now getting started on the cookies."

"Cookies, sir?" Moving to follow him out, I almost ran directly into him as he stopped abruptly and turned a glare at me.

"Don't sir me. I might be a senator, but I'm not ancient. Call me William." Shaking his head, he turned back around and led the way to the kitchen. "And yes, cookies. Every year, those three make cookies. I have to remind myself to check the expiration date on my fire extinguisher after they managed to catch a pot on fire a couple of years ago trying to make a caramel drizzle."

"And now I know why she always lets me cook," I laughed, shaking my head. Distantly, I heard something fall followed by the girls screeching. "Sounds like we need to go supervise."

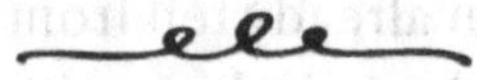

After dinner, and many cookies, William called all of the girls over so that he could give them their gifts. I learned throughout the day that they have formed traditions. Supervised cookies followed by Christmas Eve dinner catching up and laughing with one another, and then he gives them their gifts and they give him his. The girls wait until Christmas day to have their gift exchange, which they would be including me in.

Sitting on the other end of the sectional, I watched as the girls all sat on the coffee table in front of him; Charlotte on the left, Ingrid in the middle, and Desiree on the right. It was clear that he loved the girls as if they were his own, and took the time to genuinely know them. It was sweet to see, especially since I knew she viewed them as her soul sisters.

"You first, Charlotte," he said as he handed her over a small gift wrapped in sunshine yellow paper with a green bow. She opened it carefully and it looked to be seeds of some kind. "These were her mother's favorite flowers. I'm sure you have plenty of daisies, but the world could always use some more and I know nobody else more perfect to grow them." Charlotte sniffled and leaned forward to give him a hug and whispered something to him that I couldn't hear.

He cleared his throat, composing himself, and turned to Desiree. "Now for you." She received another small package, wrapped in pale blue with a white ribbon tied around it. The item was tucked into a box and I couldn't see the contents from where I was sitting on the couch. "I know Ingrid will forgive me for giving these to you, but these were a few of her mom's favorite pieces. There's a necklace, a pair of earrings, a couple of rings, and a bracelet. You have my permission to either leave them as is or completely deconstruct them into something different. I know they're safe in your hands."

I watched as the two of them shared a moment and I didn't miss the excited determination gleam in Desiree's eyes as she silently vowed not to let him down. He threw her a wink and a mischievous smile that reminded me of how my dad and I interacted from time to time when we were up to no good.

"And lastly, for my darling Ingrid." He shifted so that he was facing directly in front of him. Her gift was a small, lilac envelope with a pink ribbon. When she opened it with delicate fingers, it looked like a scrap of fabric was hiding inside. "As you know, years ago I donated your mother's wedding dress to one of the local hospitals for it to be turned into baby gowns in the NICU. Before I did that, however, I cut a small piece from the bustle and had it made into a handkerchief for you. The words on it are in her handwriting from one of the letters she wrote to you before you were born."

Ingrid's breath caught and I watched as Desiree and Charlotte both leaned their heads on each of her shoulders. All three of them seemed to be silently crying together over the sheer amount of thought he put into each of their gifts. Even with them all being tied to her mom in some way, you could tell those were his way of keeping her memory alive while still being able to spread his love to those around him.

After the four of them shared a hug, the girls each made their way back over to the couch. Once Ingrid was next to me, I brought her into my arms and kissed her gently on the top of her head. She was clutching the fabric in her hands and eventually held it up for me to see. In the corner, a simple "I love you" was stitched in light blue thread.

As the night progressed, I learned about the rest of their Christmas Eve traditions. It turned out, after the gift exchange, everybody snuggled into the couch to watch Christmas movies, drink hot cocoa, and eat more cookies.

Halfway through *How the Grinch Stole Christmas*, Desiree excused herself to refill her mug and I took the opportunity to follow her to the kitchen, making sure not to disturb Ingrid as she slept.

"Hey, Desiree, can I talk to you for a sec?" I asked once I caught up with her.

She set her mug down and shot me a sly grin. "Absolutely. I figured you'd come to see me at some point."

"Well, who else is going to make her engagement ring?"

"I'm glad to see that you know there's only one correct answer to that question. I already have you penciled in after the new years. I think we might actually be able to do something with the rings William gave me today." As she spoke, her face lit up with excitement as her brain started thinking about all of the possibilities.

"Fantastic," I said. "I managed to get hers and Charlotte's cards but didn't get yours. I'm assuming your number is on your website, yeah? Can I give you a call next week to set up a real appointment?"

"Sounds good to me. With the new year being a week from now, give me a call on the 30th."

With that set in motion, I grabbed a couple of cookies for myself and Ingrid, sure she would wake up once she heard me munching, and made my way back to the couch. It was probably too soon for me to already be thinking about the ring, but I wanted it to be perfect, and perfection took time. Time was not something we had when I planned on proposing to my little minx in two and a half months.

"Hey," Ingrid murmured, nose scrunched as she sat up a little to look at me once I sat back down. "Whatcha got there?"

Chuckling to myself, I pulled a cookie out from where I had it hiding behind my back and she made grabby hands as I passed it over to her.

Seventeen

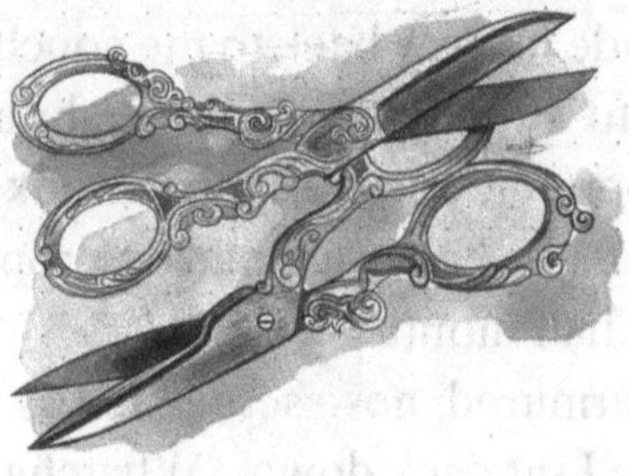

Ingrid

I woke up on Christmas morning to a loud banging on the bedroom door. The girls were yelling for us to get up for breakfast and Josh groaned beside me as he pulled me closer into his chest.

"Make. Them. Stop." His growls in my ear sent chills racing down my arms. Somehow, he pulled me even closer to him and I felt my back arch as he nuzzled his face into my neck and started laying lazy kisses on my skin. If it weren't for the incessant pounding on the door, I would have let him continue his exploration.

But alas...

"Get up, bitch!" I heard Char yell. "I'm giving you both five seconds to be decent and then I'm storming in there!"

Josh and I shared an "oh fuck" look. Within a blink, he pulled the blanket up until the only part of me not covered was my nose up, him somehow hidden completely underneath.

"Josh, get out from under there or it will appear very *indecent*," I whisper yelled.

"Oh, good! Maybe it'll make them leave the moment they walk in."

Before he could even finish his sentence, they burst through the door. Without a care in the world, they dropped onto the bed, Char landing directly on top of Josh.

"This mattress is lumpier than I remember," she mused as she wiggled her ass and made little jump movements to get comfortable.

"Get. Off," Josh growled, completely smushed beneath her. Unable to stifle the laughter, I reached for my sweater on the floor by the bed and managed to get it on while staying covered as Char moved to sit by Desi toward the end of the bed. When Josh wiggled his way out from under the comforter, he frowned as he looked at me. "Dammit, now she's dressed."

"Look, I understand you're new around here, but it's breakfast time," Desi explained. She was looking at him like she was daring him to argue with her about our traditions.

Maybe I shouldn't have gotten her new wire cutters this year.

"She's right," I told him, nodding my head. He looked flat out betrayed which just made me laugh more. "We can't open presents until after we eat. So, unless you want me to return your gift..." Excitedly, he jumped out of bed, somehow in boxers that were *definitely* not there prior to the girls entering the room, and started racing to put on his Christmas pajamas.

"Well, what're we waiting for? Let's go!"

Desi and Char looked at me while laughing their heads off. The three of us wore matching pjs every year and because Josh joined us, he got to match, too. This year, they were covered in dinosaurs wearing Santa hats. I made a promise to the girls that we would be out soon and made to put on my own once they left.

"You didn't have to get me a gift, little minx," I heard Josh say as I was buttoning my shirt. His brows were pushed together and he had a small frown on his face. "You giving me this chance to be with you was more than I expected as it is."

"Shut up, Josh," I said with my hands on my hips. "It's Christmas. You're my boyfriend. I got you a gift. Now, do you want it or would you prefer I return it?"

The smile returned to his face and he nodded his head as his anxieties melted away. "I want it."

"Good boy." The look then turned to one that I knew meant I would be in for it later. I laughed and started backing away before he could swat my ass. "No time! Let's go before the girls kill us!"

After breakfast, which Josh ended up taking over cooking because *apparently* the three of us couldn't be trusted, we all gathered around the tree in the living room and sat on the floor. My dad claimed his seat in the chair by the fireplace and looked every bit the part of a proud parent with the Santa hat on his head.

"Dad first!" I exclaimed, clapping with excitement to see him open his gifts. I wasn't kidding when I told Quinn that my favorite part of the holidays was seeing everybody's reactions to what they got. I heard Josh chuckle behind me as we all went to hand dad his presents. Saving mine for last, he opened the others first. He got a bottle of brandy from Josh, a book on understanding modern lingo from Char, new gold cufflinks from Desi, before finally getting to the new royal purple tie from me. He got up with a dramatic grunt and gave each of us hugs, sans Josh, who got a handshake, and promised he loved each item.

Moving on, the girls and I had our little exchange. Char told me she'd been needing new gloves and decided to just wear her gift, claiming she needed to break them in. Desi loved her new wire cutters and made sure Josh heard her when she practically drooled over how sharp they were and would be like cutting through butter. I received a stunning set of sewing needles from Char and one of my fancy sketch pads that I never let myself splurge on from Desi. Once the girls started exchanging their gifts to each other, Josh and I started our little exchange.

"Should we open at the same time?" He asked, placing his hand on my knee just because he could.

"Absolutely not, the reaction to the gift is the best part!

"Okay fine," He laughed and booped me on the nose. "Would you like to go first?"

"Nope, I've been waiting too long to see you open yours," I said firmly as I shook my head no. I watched as he *slowly* unwrapped his gift, still laughing to himself at my very serious gift giving rules. Once he opened it, however, his laughter came to a complete stop. He held the mug carefully in his hands, testing the weight of it, as he looked over all of the small details. I fidgeted with my hands as he ran a thumb over the handle. "Now you have a designated mug just for you every morning. I thought once we inevitably move, our mugs can sit next to each other on display about a new coffee bar."

His head popped up, eyes searching mine like he was trying to figure out if I was serious about what I was saying. I knew what the gift meant. It meant I already knew what we would decide once the three months were up. It meant I'd made my decision about whether or not we would remain in each other's lives. I gave him a genuine smile and a slight nod of my head, wishing I had a camera ready to see the way his whole face lit up. His eyes had a glassy look to them and I could tell he was trying with all of his might not to let the tears fall. "Thank you, little minx. This is perfect."

"My turn?" I asked and he cleared his throat as he nodded his head. He handed me my gift and it was in a small, thin box. I tried shaking it to guess the contents, causing him to laugh again, but that gave nothing away. Carefully opening it, I saw a lilac passport holder with gold foil detailing nestled inside. When I took it out of the tin, I was shocked that it felt like something else was inside of it and when I opened it up, I gasped. "How did you–"

"You had done most of the leg work for it already, actually. I managed to find the folder when I was looking at your knick knack shelf that had everything you needed for the passport. I just needed your ID and a photo. Wes and I worked together to find a picture of you that met the requirements. Luckily, one of the dresses from the winter line that you modeled was perfect. He was able to crop it and get it formatted right so that it could be used for your passport. Then, I just snagged your ID and went and submitted your application. I managed to convince them to put in a rush order for it."

His eyes roamed over me as I examined the gift. I kept meaning to get the application submitted, I just couldn't find the time to go in and get the passport photo. I never thought about just using one I already had. I felt a tear drip off of my face and I quickly moved my gift away to avoid crying on it.

"I figured, if all goes as planned, you're going to need it soon," he continued and I finally met his eyes, tears streaming down my face. Our honeymoon. He got me a passport so that we could go somewhere far away for our honeymoon.

This man, this unbelievably incredible man.

I set the passport back in its box and crawled over to him and climbed into his lap, hugging him tight. I needed to say thank you, but I couldn't get the words out past my tears. He murmured sweet words in my ear as he let me cry while he held me and planted kisses in my hair.

"I love you," I hiccuped once I stopped being a blubbering mess. "Thank you so much."

"I love you, too, little minx. Now can we go sit somewhere more comfortable? My ass is numb." I let out a watery laugh while I stood to haul him up off of the floor.

The rest of the day went by perfectly. We watched more holiday movies, ate cookies, played games and just spent the day enjoying each other's company. My dad managed to stay in his chair most of the day while he read over the book Char had given him. It couldn't have been a better Christmas if we tried.

Eighteen

Joshua

The girls all said their goodbyes to William and made their way to the SUV. Getting to spend the Christmas weekend with them was incredible. Hell, life in general had been incredible ever since I met Ingrid. I watched as she hugged her dad one last time before she climbed into the passenger seat. William and I stood next to each other as we watched them laugh about something and I could vaguely see Desiree try to pry the gardening gloves off of Charlotte's hands. Ingrid couldn't stop laughing and I could have sworn I heard hers all the way from the front door.

"They really are something else, aren't they?" He asked, shaking his head. "When she brought those two into our lives, I didn't anticipate them becoming something like daughters for me."

"I can tell they love you almost as much as they love her." Ingrid explained to me why the girls joined her for the holidays every year. It didn't surprise me in the slightest that the girl who grew up with only one parent would want to make sure they weren't alone during the holiday season.

"They like you, too, you know." I turned to look at him and saw him already staring at me, arms crossed and a smug look on his face. "Well, are you going to ask?"

Taking a deep breath, I turned so that my whole body was facing him, hoping that I looked more confident than I felt. "In the beginning of March, I'm hoping to propose to Ingrid, so long as she wants to keep me around. I'm working with Desiree to create her engagement ring, however nothing official has begun yet. I gave your daughter a passport for Christmas because I know her dream is to travel and I want to take her all over the world. I want to make her the happiest woman to ever walk this earth."

He said he wouldn't interrogate me and so I just decided to word vomit? What the fuck, *Josh.*

"While I understand and respect that you're a traditional man, I appreciate that you don't fault myself or Ingrid in our very untraditional arrangement we have. I hope to give her every wish she has ever wanted and fulfill every dream by her side, but I can't do that without first asking you for your blessing. So, William, may I have your blessing in asking your incredible daughter to be my wife?"

I forced myself to maintain eye contact as he made me wait for his answer.

I should have just asked without all of the extra information. How much do I need his blessing, anyways?

I love Ingrid. I don't need her father's permission to marry her, right?

Why is he just staring *at me?*

Fuck can he tell I'm panic—

"You have my blessing," he finally said, interrupting my inner turmoil. I let out a heavy sigh of relief as I nodded my head and held my hand out to shake his.

God dammit, this isn't a fucking business deal.

"Thank you. I promise I'll keep her happy."

"Yeah, yeah. Do me a favor would you?" I nodded for him to continue. "Get her to move out from above her shop. It's unsafe and I don't like that it encourages her lack of a work/life balance."

Shaking my head with a light chuckle, I said, "Believe me, I agree. We'll need to move to a bigger place sooner, anyways. I'm currently working with a quarter of my belongings." I'd already planned to bring that up with her over the next couple of weeks. We needed to make a game plan sooner rather than later. William and I said our goodbyes and when I got into the driver's seat, the girls were discussing work.

"So, you two seemed to have a productive conversation," Ingrid mused as she nudged my side.

I put on my seatbelt as I played nonchalant. "We did."

"And?" Her eyes narrowed, her nose doing the scrunchy thing that I loved.

"We were discussing whether or not we should get you three baking classes so that we don't have to fear for our lives next year," I lied as I booped her nose just because I could.

She huffed and turned to face the windshield, arms crossed over her chest as she scowled. "Uh-huh. Sure."

Because the finance world didn't understand the concept of a holiday season, I was back in the office the day after we got back home. I could usually work from home but on days with endless meetings, it's easier to just be at the office for them. Checking my calendar before heading off to the next one, I saw that my assistant had added a gala for an animal conservation charity at the end of January. I found the correlating email and saw that Julian had already taken care of the RSVP, but he neglected to mark that I would have a plus one.

"Hey, Julian?" I stopped at his desk on my way toward the conference room. "I see you didn't include a plus one for me for the *Wild Haven* Gala. Are you able to get this corrected? I'll be bringing my girlfriend, Ingrid Morgan."

"Oh, my apologies, sir," he said, a confused look on his face. "Your mother is the one who sent over the information and didn't include that you would be allowed a plus one. I'll reach out to the gala directly to have this corrected."

For fuck's sake. Mom seemed to be taking this further than I thought she would. She was going to need to get over whatever reasoning she had for not liking Ingrid.

Wanting to make sure I let Ingrid know, I shot her a text to double check that she'd be able to go.

> Hey, little minx. I have a proposition for you.

Minx

> Oh boy, let's hear it.

> I have to go to a charity gala at the end of January. I know you'll be busy with getting started on sewing the spring line, but I was wondering if you could spare an evening and go with me?

Quickly getting the information sent over to her, I pocketed my phone as I walked into the conference room. So far, only myself and my father had arrived.

"Hey dad, perfect. I actually wanted to talk to you for a second." We had a few minutes before the rest of the group would make it in and I needed to talk to him about what my mother had been up to.

"What's going on, son? Is everything okay? You left in a hurry at the party."

"I take it mom didn't fill you in on the details of *why* we dipped out early?" He shook his head, concern etched in the lines on his face. "She decided to attack Ingrid at the party, saying her mother must have failed her in not teaching her how to be a proper housewife. You know, the same mother that has been dead since Ingrid was born." I watched as his shoulders slumped, arms dangling at his side and his eyes widened.

"I'm sure she didn't mean that, she—"

"I heard the conversation, dad. On top of this, I just received the information for the gala in January and mom deliberately left out the possibility of me having a plus one."

"I see," he said, nodding like he understood my question before I could even ask it. "Did Senator Morgan give you his blessing?"

"He did. Don't worry, I made sure to tell him that he had your vote," I laughed before getting serious once more. "I need you to talk to mom. Ingrid wants a relationship with her. I think she was hoping to finally have a mom. That won't happen if mom continues to treat her like this." He nodded his head as the rest of the group started filtering into the room.

Nineteen

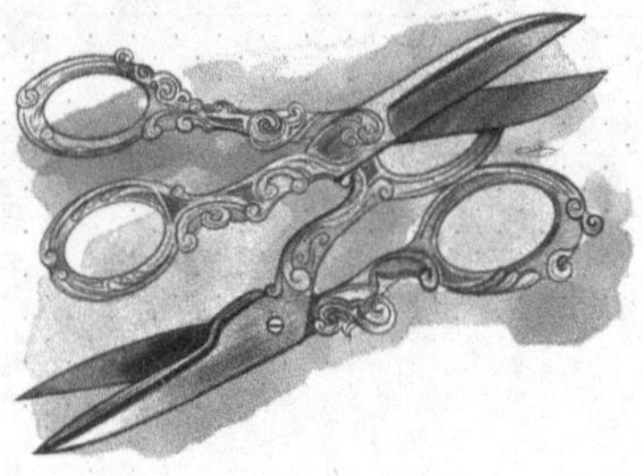

Ingrid

"Ooo, what about this one?" Josh brought up looking for a place for the two of us to move into after the three months were up and I was grateful that he had. I'd be lying if I said that I wasn't starting to stress about when we could finally talk about it, and if bringing it up would have been too soon.

We were looking at places together and I may have found the perfect one. Most of what we looked at, the commute wouldn't work well for him for days he needed to go in, were in a rougher area, or were too far from my shop. We decided that, for now, we wanted to get a home on the island and later down the line see about getting some vacation homes elsewhere.

"Is that a double island?" Josh peered over my shoulder to look at the listing I had pulled up.

"Yes! Just think, you can use the other island for dishes and presenting family style and then we can use the second island to actually eat at," I explained, using my hands to try to paint the picture for him. "Look! It even has a coffee nook!"

"Go ahead and send it over so I can have our realtor take a look," he said with a look of excitement in his eyes as I continued scrolling through the pictures. This house would be perfect. It wasn't too far so I wouldn't need to relocate my business, and Josh would even be able to have a home office space.

Once we started discussing what we were looking for in our home, it got easier with weeding out the ones we knew we didn't want. We'd only been looking for a few days seeing as our timeline was on warp speed, but we wanted to have a house ready to go by the end of the February so that we could start the next phase of our relationship somewhere that was entirely *us*. If this house ended up having a big yard, I truly believed I managed to find our future home.

While I sent him the listing, he stepped outside to make a work call. It was the 30th, so he was trying to make sure he took care of everything he needed before the New Years Eve party we had planned for the next day. I couldn't wait to have all of our friends finally spend time together and meet. I was also secretly hoping the party would convince Wes to finally make a move with Char.

As though the girls could tell I was thinking about them, my phone buzzed on the couch next to me with a notification for the group chat.

So, I'm definitely going to need both of your help with picking an outfit for tomorrow. Is there a dress code? Should I look cute? Should I be comfy? HELP

There isn't a dress code, you goob. Just wear your cute jeans with the tears in them, your black sparkly long sleeve and your boots!

Char

How the fuck did you do that? In my best Rory Gilmore impression, I've been staring at that top for 20 minutes!

Are you nervous for tomorrow? I promise it'll be very chill, just us three and Josh and his guys.

Char

Me? Nervous? Pfft… YES! What if the reason Wes hasn't asked me out yet is actually because he isn't even into me?!

As much as I know that isn't true, he would be an idiot if he wasn't into you. But again, he IS into you, so you don't need to worry about that!

Oh! Can you two come over early tomorrow to help me set up? Then we can get ready together, too!

Char

Yeah, I can swing that! Desi, can you bring me some jewelry options pretty please? Nothing I have is making sense and I've decided to simply give up and let you take the wheel on that.

Just then, Josh walked in with a mischievous grin on his face and a little pep in his step as he walked into the kitchen to start making us lunch.

Weird way to be after a work *call...*

Char

Desiiiiiiii please!!!

Desi

Sorry! I was with a customer! Yes, I will bring over all of the things for you. Hey Ingrid, unrelated, is Carlisle also single?

I hollered over my shoulder, "Hey babe, Carlisle is single, right? I haven't heard you mention anything about him dating anybody."

"Yeah, he's single. Why?" He walked over to see who I was texting. "Oh no, are we just going to have our entire wedding party fucking at this point?"

"Would it be bad if we did?" I asked, genuinely curious to see if it would be a problem if all of our friends ended up together.

"Honestly? This may be the best case scenario. I am curious to see how Desi and Carlisle would get along."

Just checked with Josh, he's single! But at least meet the guy first before you get any crazy ideas lol

Desi

Yeah yeah. Anyways, I'll come over early, as well! Can't wait to ring in the new year with my favorite bitches

As I went back to looking at house listings, Josh walked up behind me and closed my laptop while placing a panini in front of me and kissed my cheek. "Eat, please. I have a meal of my own I am *dying* to eat but I need to wait until you've finished your own meal."

A shiver ran down my spine as I looked up at him. Trying to change the subject, I said, "Did your work call go alright? You can take those in here, you know. I don't mind."

"I know, little minx. But we were house hunting and I didn't want to taint that excitement with work stuff." He planted a kiss on top of my head and I melted into his touch. "The call went well. I'm going to have a few extra meetings coming up to help close this deal I'm working on. I'm a little excited about it, it could mean big things for the future. Now, eat, little minx. I'm starving and you're taking too long."

With that, he walked around the couch to kneel in front of me, leaning on my knees as he picked up the panini and hand fed me. He continued this until my plate was clean before moving the plate to the side.

"Good girl, Ingrid. Now it's my turn."

And just like that, the dress I was wearing was above my waist and his head was between my legs, doing exactly what he said he was going to do. Eat lunch.

"Knock knock, bitch!" Char yelled as she and Desi both walked through the front door after using one of their keys to get it. "We're here to get hot and party our asses off!"

Startled, I yelped with alarm and started falling off of the barstool I was standing on to help Josh hang the streamers.

"Fuck! Ingrid, hang on!" Josh managed to catch me right as the stool moved completely out from under my feet. Distantly, I could see the streamer roll I was holding arch in the air as I somehow managed to throw it. I landed in his arms with an *oomph* and couldn't help but laugh at myself. Josh, however, still looked alarmed and his eyes scanned over my body while I felt his heart race in his chest. "You okay, little minx?"

Both girls immediately started apologizing and I waved them off, still laughing to the point I had tears in my eyes. "Girls, it's fine! I'm fine!" I wiped my eyes and tried to calm myself down and looked up at Josh, booping his nose. "Thanks for catching me, sweetheart."

"Like I would ever let you just fall on your ass," he said matter of factly before giving me a kiss and putting me back on the ground. "Alight ladies, now that you have officially caused some chaos, can you three finish with the decorations while I work on the food?"

We managed to get the rest of the decorations done without further issue. Once the streamers were all put up, we added a makeshift photobooth set up with silly glasses and party blowers at the edge of the room. After my apartment was sufficiently covered in glitter, we left Josh to his own devices in the kitchen to go get ready.

"So, are you ready to see Wes?" I asked Char. We were doing the finishing touches on our hair and makeup before changing into our outfits for the night. Char seemed to have calmed down some more since the day before, but that may have had to do with the champagne we'd been drinking since camping out in my bedroom.

"Yeah, I'm hoping that a social setting with both of our friends will help us break the ice," she said as she applied a coat of mascara.

"Well, I for one am excited to meet the third friend," Desi interjected while almost tripping putting her tights on. "Shit!"

"You've gotta stop referring to him as 'the third friend'." I threw a pillow at her hip to emphasize my point, throwing her off balance again.

She steadied herself and huffed. "Fine, I'm excited to meet *Carlisle*. What kind of pretentious name is Carlisle Du Pont, anyways?"

"Girl, I know you're not judging. You both have fancy French names," Char said, causing all of us to laugh as Desi clasped a necklace around her neck.

The two of them continued going back and forth over what made a name pretentious while I continued getting ready. We had to get ready in my room since the bathroom really wasn't big enough for all three of us. I'd never thought much about how little space I've allowed myself over the years, but now all I could think about was how much fun it would be to have parties and girls nights once Josh and I moved. It must have shown on my face how lost in thought I was, because suddenly I was the one being hit with a stray pillow.

"What are you over there thinking about?" Char asked. She was sitting on my bed, sipping more champagne.

"Just future stuff. Josh and I started house hunting."

Both of their eyes widened, but Desi was the one to speak first. "So this is really happening then? You two might actually get married?"

I pulled at my fingers, suddenly nervous. "Is it crazy to admit that I really hope so? I didn't realize how much love I was missing out on before, but now that I have his, I don't want to lose it. Sure, our situation is unconventional, but... I've never been this happy."

Next thing I knew, I was being pushed toward the ground as both of them flew at me for a group hug. We were all laughing and I was pretty sure that was partly to cover up how misty eyed we'd all gotten.

"Okay, okay!" I pushed them both off of me. "Enough of this. Let's finish getting ready so we can get out there. I'm pretty sure the guys just walked in."

After a few touch ups, we finally made our way out into the living room. The guys all stopped their conversation and turned in our direction at the sound of our heels on the hardwood flooring.

A few things happened all in the span of mere seconds. First, Josh looked at me with the biggest smile on his face and hunger in his eyes. Second, Wesley's morphed into a sheepish grin as he caught Charlotte's eye. Lastly, Carlisle's face went from stoic to like he'd seen a ghost at the same time I heard Desiree mutter "shit" under her breath.

Twenty

Joshua

The girls were singing karaoke in the living room when I felt my phone buzz in my pocket. The guys and I were in the kitchen, drinking beer, and admiring the girls from afar. Something was going on between Carlisle and Desiree, but no matter what I tried, he wasn't budging. From the way Ingrid kept eyeing her friend, I had to assume she was getting the same non answer that I was.

Luckily, Wes and Charlotte seemed to be breaking the ice between them. Even with whatever was going on, both of my friends hadn't let the girls want for anything all night. Even if it meant Carlisle had a pissed off look on his face when he switched out Desiree's champagne for water. Wes, on the other hand, looked like a puppy as he trailed after Charlotte.

My beer was halfway to my mouth when I felt my phone buzz again. This time, it was a consistent buzzing to let me know I was getting a phone call. Sighing, I pulled my phone out to see it was my realtor. I quickly excused myself, passing my beer off to one of the guys for a moment, and ran toward the front door.

"Josh! Where are you going?" I heard Ingrid shout while trying not to stumble over the coffee table to get to me.

"I'll be right back, just have to take this call." She scrunched her nose at me and pouted, but I didn't have time to kiss it off. "Don't give me that look, little minx. Have fun, this won't take me very long."

Answering the phone as I closed the door behind me, I sighed in relief at the sound of Greg's voice on the other line. He sounded almost out of breath as he said, *"Oh thank God, I was worried I wouldn't be able to get ahold of you given the holiday."*

"Is everything okay?" I asked, getting straight to the point.

"I was able to get a response from the owners of that house you put an offer on yesterday," he rushed to respond, clearly understanding that I needed our conversation to go quickly.

I took a look over my shoulder to confirm nobody followed me outside before I said, "And? Don't tell me they already decided on another buyer."

"They did decide on a buyer. They decided on you. They're good to go to close on the house whenever you're ready." I could hear the excitement in his tone as he continued, *"Obviously, we need to go through all of the inspections first, but it should pass with flying colors. You should be good to start moving your stuff into the house within the next couple of weeks."*

"Are you messing with me, Greg? Why did they approve it so quickly? Is there something wrong with the house?" As excited as I was, I wasn't expecting to get an offer accepted that fast, let alone one willing to close fast.

"From what I understand, they're just wanting to get out of the house quickly because they're moving down south. They've already begun that process and want to tie up loose ends here so they don't have to worry about them."

I guess that made sense. Greg assured me that he had everything taken care of for the inspections and would let me know if there were any hiccups. Once we hung up, I schooled my features to make sure Ingrid couldn't tell I was up to something.

Carlisle passed me my drink as I entered the kitchen. I would need to let Desiree know about my plan and could trust that she would get Charlotte on board, but for the time being, I could bring the guys in the loop.

"That wasn't a work call, was it?" Carlisle asked with a knowing smile.

"No, it wasn't. Any chance you two could help me with getting the penthouse emptied out?"

Wes and Carlisle both looked at me with a mixture of confusion and concern before Wes piped in. "I mean, of course we can, but where are we putting everything? Manhattan isn't really the place for a garage sale."

"I just got off the phone with my realtor," I told them, making sure to keep my posture nonchalant. I couldn't tell them everything I wanted to because even though I knew she couldn't hear me, I could feel her eyes on my back.

They both slowly smiled and with a nod of my head, I redirected the conversation by looking at my watch. "Five minutes until midnight, everybody!"

The girls had stopped with their singing and switched the TV over to show the live stream of the ball drop. We may have lived in New York, but we had zero desire to be around that many people in Times Square.

As I walked over to Ingrid, I turned the main lights off so that only the twinkle lights we hung were lit, making the room look blanketed in stars. She immediately wedged herself into my side where I draped my arm over her shoulders and kissed the top of her head.

"Are you excited for the new year, little minx?" I asked as I gripped her chin between my fingers to tilt her head up. Her eyes met mine, still a little glassy from the champagne. I switched her to water earlier with the promise of one more glass when the ball dropped, and I was pleased to see she was mostly clear headed. I had plans for her, after all.

Because I couldn't help myself, I brought my hand from her chin and snaked it under her hair at the nape of her neck, tugging just a little. I marveled at the way her pupils blew, overtaking her hazel eyes, as her tongue darted out to lick her lips. She seemed to have forgotten I'd asked her a question and responded with just a noncommittal hum.

"Oh, I'm sure the year will bring plenty of whatever that pretty little head of yours is thinking," I promised, tugging her hair just a little harder. "You need to drink just a little more water, though, if you're hoping to bring any of those thoughts to life tonight." The heat in her eyes faded just a touch as she pouted.

"You switched me to water forever ago and I've only snuck a *little* champagne from the girls." Her nose was scrunched as her face twisted into a pout. She was trying so hard to be stern, but I could still see the amusement in her eyes even in the dim light.

"Hmm." I leaned closer so my mouth was next to her ear before saying, "Then it looks like we'll be able to kick them out sooner than I anticipated."

Just then, the crowd on the TV started the countdown from ten. Out of the corner of my eye, I saw Wes next to Charlotte, looking at her not much different from how I was sure I looked at my own girl. Desiree and Carlisle seemed to have disappeared, but they were probably just in the kitchen grabbing a drink.

Five

"It's going to be an adventure, little minx. Are you sure you're ready?"

Four

"I've never been more ready for anything, Joshua Astor the Third."

Three

"I sure hope you mean that, because I have plans for you."

Two

I tilted her head some with the leverage I still held from my hand in her hair.

One

She arched her back ever so slightly, pressing into me more.

HAPPY NEW YEAR!

I kissed her like nobody else was there. No, that wasn't quite right. I kissed her like the whole world *was* there. It was a claiming kiss. A promise. I kissed her like if I stopped, she would disappear, but not without knowing she would always belong in my arms. I could vaguely still hear the cheering on the TV and our friends laughed and blew noise makers. I didn't care about any of it.

Just this moment. Just *her*.

I pecked her on the lips one last time before I bent down and threw her over my shoulder.

"Happy New Year, guys! With zero respect or shame, the party is officially over." I turned in place to locate both of my guys as Ingrid squealed behind me. "You two, get the girls home please. I'm trusting you both with their safety. Otherwise, I can't promise my future wife here won't cut you with her fabric shears."

I watched as Wes walked Charlotte outside, both of them laughing at my ridiculousness as he did his best to keep her steady. Carlisle and Desiree looked decidedly pissed as they alternated between glaring at me and glaring at each other. He had his hand on her elbow and was trying to guide her as she stumbled and I could hear her telling him she's fine. As much as I wanted to figure out what was going on between them, I couldn't be bothered right then. I trusted him to get her home and I *mostly* trusted her not to stab him.

With my little minx still kicking and squealing as she tried to shout goodbyes at them, I made sure the front door was locked before I carried her bratty ass to the bedroom to make good on those promises I made to her earlier.

Twenty-One

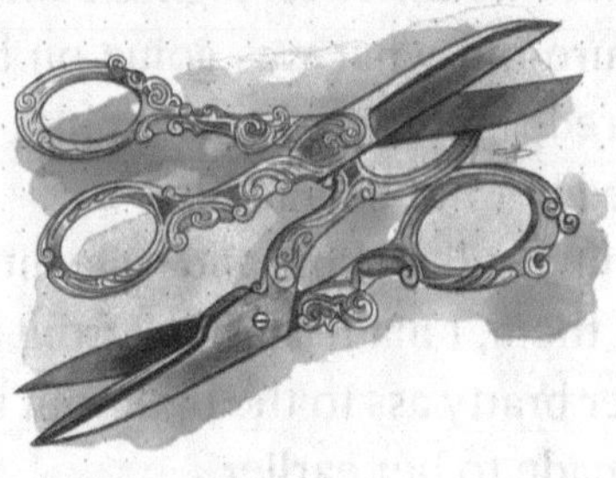

Ingrid

I landed on the bed with a plop and watched as Josh walked over to me. He wasted no time in getting my sparkly dress off of me, but when he saw what was underneath, his hands stilled.

"Little minx, what's this?" My back arched on instinct at the feel of his fingertips on my skin and along the edge of my garter belt.

"I know we have rules in this house, but I've been working on some pieces for a potential honeymoon," I said coyly. "Do you like them? These are just prototypes."

His wide eyes tracked my movements as I brought my hands up to the straps on the delicate bra. The entire set was black lace with embroidered flowers scattered. His lids started to droop with desire as I grabbed his hand and brought it toward my center.

"I was hoping that maybe we could compromise," I said as I continued my movements, letting his hand move closer to the slit in my crotchless panties. "Does this still count as easy access?" I shifted so that my heels were on the mattress, my thighs spread wide, so that he could get a clear view of what I made for him.

He dropped to his knees so fast, I worried for a moment he may have hurt himself. He didn't even seem to notice as he squared his shoulders between my stilettos, eyes honed in on my dripping cunt. I couldn't even tell if he was still breathing. He may not have been.

Without saying a word, he brought his arms under my legs and grabbed my ass with both hands to bring me directly to his mouth.

"Josh!"

He was showing no mercy as he alternated between sucking on my clit and plunging his tongue deep inside me, his grip on my ass getting stronger the more my body started winding up to the orgasm I was already on the cusp of. He unlatched from my clit and plunged two fingers inside of me to massage my g-spot.

"Am I allowed to rip any of this?" He was pressing his thumb directly on my clit as he asked.

I didn't know why he thought I could answer any question, so instead of answering like I intended to, I just made some kind of noise as the pressure grew stronger. When he noticed my struggle, he stopped all movement.

"Ingrid, am I allowed to rip any of this?" He asked one more time.

"I made them for you to destroy," I managed to say breathlessly.

That seemed to be all the permission he needed. Next thing I knew, his hand was out of me and back to gripping my ass as he lifted me up and dropped me further onto the bed. He quickly stripped out of his own clothes before he climbed onto the bed.

"Do you have any idea how beautifully stunning you are?" He crawled toward me in a predatory way before I felt his hands latching onto the lace covering my full breasts. "I know you want me to ruin this but the more I look at it, the more I don't think I can. You're so incredibly talented and I just know whatever else that brilliant mind has come up with will be just as beautiful."

He managed to find the front clasp on the bra and tossed it to the side once he took it off of me. I let him position me however he wanted as he wrapped my legs around his hips. He hadn't removed my heels, so I knew the points dug into his back as I tried to bring him closer to me. He hissed at the contact but I could feel his dick throb against me when I pressed harder.

"Josh, please. Touch me. Fuck me. *Anything.*"

He sat up so that my hips were resting on the tops of his thighs, ensuring that he still had the perfect view of him fucking me once he started. "I'm not going to be easy on you tonight, little minx," he promised.

"Good, I don't want you to be."

The moment my consent left my lips, he entered me without hesitation and holy *fuck* he was *deep*. The angle he had me at I felt like I could feel him in my throat. He moved my ankles up by his head, making it an even tighter fit, and placed his large hand on my lower abdomen. I, as always, lost any ability to speak outside of nonsensical words and moans.

I could feel myself getting closer to that precipice, but it felt different. It felt stronger and like something I didn't know I could handle.

"Josh, I–"

"Give it to me, Ingrid." His command immediately soothed the rising panic I was feeling and I felt him press slightly harder on my pelvis. "Now!"

Just as I let go, he pulled out of me and brought my hips up to his face so that most of my lower body was hovering over him and the bed. He buried his face into my pussy and lapped up my release like a man deprived.

Holy shit, did I just—

Before I could think more about it, he flipped me over with expert skill and pushed back inside me. His hand wrapped around the back of my neck to keep my face in the pillow.

"More, Ingrid. I need *more*."

He wasn't holding back as he continued to ram into me from behind. His grip on my hip combined with the pressure he was putting on my neck was punishing, teetering the blissful line between pleasure and pain. I knew he could feel my body getting closer and closer to another orgasm when he removed the hand on my neck and snaked it around to pinch my clit. *Hard*.

"Fuck, Josh!"

He kept fucking me through my orgasm as he took the same hand from my clit and brought his thumb directly to my mouth.

"Suck."

And who was I to question his intentions? I let him bring his thumb into my mouth and I sucked just as he instructed, curling my tongue around it and scraping the pad with my teeth ever so slightly. Before I could do any more, he removed it and brought his hand toward my ass. Without warning, I felt him spit directly onto my asshole before he circled his thumb over the tight hole.

"I won't take you here today, but just know I do plan to consume you in every place I can."

My body tightened just a little at the slight pressure as he slowly inserted his thumb all the way to the knuckle, immediately triggering a third orgasm.

"Good fucking girl, Ingrid," he crooned. "Fuck, keep squeezing me just like that."

His thrusts became more erratic as he removed the hand from my hip and the thumb from my ass to bring me up to his chest, one of his hands at my throat. He placed his other arm tight around my middle to keep me pressed completely against him as he bit down on the sensitive skin between my neck and my shoulder.

"FUCK!" He roared his release as his thrust began to slow. Bringing us both down to the mattress, we disentangled from each other before he pressed a tender kiss to my head and got up from the bed.

A few moments later, I felt him gently removing my shoes, stockings, garter belt and panties before a warm washcloth was used to clean me up and he left tender kisses on the inside of my thighs.

"Happy New Year, little minx," he muttered as he crawled in behind me to bring me tight into his arms, where I drifted to sleep with a sated smile on my face.

Twenty-Two

Joshua

"Good news, Josh! The house has passed all of the in-* spections and they're ready to close whenever you are.*" I listened to Greg over the phone as he gave me an update on the house. It'd been a couple of weeks since I'd placed the offer on it and now, all that was left was getting it ready for me and my girl.

"That's great to hear! Can they come by the office later this week to sign the papers and pass over the keys? I would do it now, but I'm headed off to another appointment at the moment," I said as I rounded the corner. I made sure Ingrid was busy with her spring collection and told her I had in person meetings. I couldn't risk her walking into Desi's store while I was there.

"I'll get it set up with your assistant. Congratulations, Josh!"

We ended our call right as I walked into *Estelle Jewels*, a little bell ringing as I entered. She managed to create a kind of eclectic vibe for her shop while still being elegant. Like Ingrid, she made custom pieces along with keeping a small stock of premade pieces for those not looking for customization. I found her sitting at her work bench in the center of the store.

"Josh! Hey!" She looked up from the piece she was working on. "I lost track of time, give me one second to put this away and grab the box of goodies for her piece. Go ahead and take a seat!"

I did as she asked and sat on the soft velvet wingback she had in front of her work bench. Earlier in the day, I checked to make sure she already had Ingrid's ring size because as much as I was willing to steal one from her collection, I wasn't willing to deal with her wrath once she noticed if I didn't get it back in time.

Desiree returned fairly quickly and was carrying the small box that William gave her for Christmas, and placed it on the surface of the bench before taking her seat across from me.

"Alright, so I already have some ideas, if you're open to hearing them?" She asked with an excited look on her face.

"I'm more than open to hearing them. All I know is it needs to scream Ingrid and *not* be a diamond." I didn't forget her comment about not liking the traditional stone after our first breakfast. That fact stuck in my head and was the first one to cross my mind any time I thought about proposing, which was constant.

"Perfect! So I was thinking, I don't want to deconstruct her mother's jewelry too much. Do you see these earrings and how it's the three small stones fanning out from each other? I want to take these and add them to this ring." She held up three smaller diamonds that were shaped like tiny pears and I instantly started panicking as those were clearly the exact stone I just mentioned Ingrid didn't want.

"Wait, those are diamonds though. She doesn't like diamonds."

She must have seen the panic on my face because she laughed a little and held out her hands in a way to try to calm me. "Don't worry! These go around the main stone. She won't mind these, I promise."

I breathed a sigh of relief and then asked, "What's the main stone going to be?"

She sat up a little straighter and I could feel the excitement radiating off of her as she brought the box of goodies closer and pulled out a ring box I didn't notice was inside. Instead of telling me outright, she simply passed the box over to me to look at myself. When I opened it up, I immediately understood her excitement.

The ring was white gold with a single light purple stone set in the center. While I didn't think the metal color complimented it very well, it was still perfect and I let Desiree know as such.

"I agree," she said. "My idea is to plate the ring in a soft rose gold which will look beautiful on her skin tone as well as compliment the color of the stone itself. Then I want to put the smaller diamonds I showed you on the edges of the marquise to look like this." She grabbed her tablet to show me the mock up she'd made.

"Desiree, this is perfect." I was awestruck at what she'd managed to see from a ring and some earrings. It wasn't too busy and was absolutely perfect for Ingrid. "What kind of stone is this?"

"It's an amethyst. William told me these pieces were some of Ellie's favorites, so to see that nestled in the mix almost made my heart stop. This is one of Ingrid's favorite stones and I've actually made her a matching necklace and earring set in the past."

"I hate that she never got to know her mom, but I hope that my own can help fill some of that space in her heart for her."

Desiree snorted but quickly recovered. I figured Ingrid had mentioned what happened at the Christmas party during the last brunch session, and it appeared I was correct in that assumption.

"I hope so, too, Josh."

We moved on to discussing timeline and payment, which she tried to say not to worry about to which I quickly shut down. Forty-five minutes later, we had a solid game plan for everything except retrieval, which meant it was time for phase two of our meeting.

"So, I need you to keep another secret from our girl," I started hesitantly.

"Oh?" She asked with an arched brow and crossed her arms over her chest.

"Did Ingrid by chance show you a house recently?"

"Double islands?" I nodded. "Yes, she showed me. She was practically jumping up and down as she made me look through the pictures while narrating what she had planned for each room. Please don't tell me it's sold already, it'll crush her." A look of panic swept over her face.

Reaching up to scratch the back of my neck, I eventually said, "Well, it *is* sold..." She threw her hands up in the air in an *oh god* gesture. I let her panic a little more before I added, "I bought it."

She immediately turned back around to face me. "What do you mean you *bought* it? She was just showing it to me on New Year's Eve."

I nodded. "I know, I placed the offer the day before. It was actually accepted that night. I'm meeting with my realtor later this week about closing on it since all of the inspections came back clear."

Her jaw dropped as she stared at me. "Why are we not telling her this?"

I stood up a little straighter and I was sure the smile on my face made me look like an evil villain of some kind.

"Because, I have a plan."

Twenty-Three

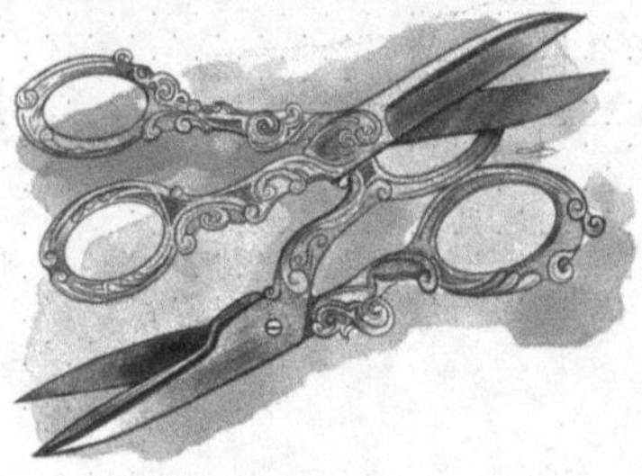

Ingrid

Josh was being weird. Like, more than usual weird. Just that morning he jumped out of bed so fast, he actually managed to wake me up, which as we all knew, was an impossible feat. I mean, he almost fell out of the bed as he practically sprinted.

If that was an isolated incident, then sure, maybe he just got extra excited to get out of bed. But he'd also been taking the majority of his phone calls out of ear shot from me, going as far as walking outside completely. He was hiding something and if it weren't for the extra love and affection he'd been giving me, I'd think there was somebody else.

I'd let him keep his secrets for the time being, since I was brewing some of my own as well, albeit I was being less obvious but... *Get it together, Josh*.

I somehow managed to get ahead of schedule with work even with the disruption to my standard day to day. I completed all of the custom orders with only a few fittings left, and I even managed to finish my sketches for the spring collection and had already started taking them from page to mannequin. Today, however, I focused on one dress in particular.

Mine.

Over the years, I'd thought about this dress more than I had any other, adding small pieces of it into every design. I knew the color, bodice, skirt, material, everything. I knew this dress as well as I knew myself, *more* than I knew myself.

Coffee in hand, I made my way downstairs to my haven. Even with Josh being in the office for a few meetings, I didn't want to risk sketching in the apartment for fear of him walking in. I had a huge tendency to lose track of time once I was working and if it weren't for him, I would honestly forget to take meal breaks most days.

Speaking of which...

> Hey love, would you mind letting me know when you're on your way home? I want to order in tonight and can place one to get here when you do

Joshua Astor (x3)

> I absolutely can, little minx. I'll give you a call when I leave.

Perfect, now I'd have time to stash the secret sketches before he pulls in!

Making sure my ringer was on, I set my phone on my desk and pulled out the *portfolio*. This one was specific just to my dress. I had fabric samples, perfume notes, clippings of shoes, basically everything except the veil and dress sketches. It'd somehow managed to turn into a wedding dream board over the years, and I kept it under lock and key at all times unless I was actively putting something in it. It even held a specific sketchbook that I didn't keep stock of purely because of how expensive it was. I was a sucker for good stationary as much as the next girl, but even I had my limits.

I turned on the shared playlist Josh and I made together and got started. As I was getting a me shaped model down onto the page, I drifted off into my own little world thinking about him and how he'd become the center of my world in such a short time.

I would love to reflect back and say that I was skeptical at first, but honestly, that would be a lie. Was it crazy for me to let him move in after a literal *day* of knowing him? Of course it was. But I couldn't bring myself to question that judgment when I thought about how much we just *worked* so well together. I'd never felt such an absolute instant connection with anybody like I did with him.

I knew I rarely took the time out of my life to really try to form bonds outside of my girls, but it wasn't like any guys had made an effort, either. Anytime we went out to bars, it was Desi and Char who were getting the attention. Not that I ever minded, but one night stands weren't something I was ever looking for. Especially not after the ghosting Desi dealt with over Halloween. Now that I thought about it, that was the last hook up she'd had, having sworn off men entirely afterwards.

My pencil drifted over the page as I started working on the overall shape and neckline for the dress and my thoughts drifted to what my mom looked like on her wedding day. I could only hope to look as beautiful as she did. Dad never got rid of any of the tapes or pictures and I looked at them all the time growing up. I liked to believe that was where my initial wedding dress fixation started. Watching her walk down the aisle toward my dad with her train and veil flowing easily behind her, but if I was being honest with myself, the dress was never what made her beautiful.

No, it was the love that shone in her eyes, the way she clung to my grandfather's arm like if she didn't then she would fall to her knees. It was the same look reflected in my father's eyes when the camera would pan to him. My parents' wedding footage was my favorite movie for the love displayed alone.

I could feel my eyes watering at the memory and quickly flipped my head back to avoid ruining the sketch just as my music stopped and my phone started ringing. Quickly, I wiped my eyes and cleared my throat so he wouldn't catch on to something being wrong.

Taking a shaky breath, I answered the phone on what must have been the last ring. "Hey sweetheart, you headed home now?"

"I sure am, little minx. You must be busy over there, I was almost worried you weren't going to answer," he said and I could hear the amusement in his tone, the smile on his face.

"Oh, you know, just in the shop making sure the dress for the gala doesn't need any tweaks," I lied easily. I'd already checked the dress the other day and as predicted, it was perfect and needed nothing.

"Oh? Do you still have it on?" He couldn't hide his hopefulness if he tried.

"Of course not. Why do you think it took so long to answer?"

I heard him curse under his breath before we jumped into getting our food taken care of and ordered. Once that was settled, I decided to swing the topic back around to the gala. I didn't necessarily want to discuss it, but it'd been eating at me.

"Hey, Josh?" I asked, with more than a little hesitancy.

"Yes, little minx?"

"About the gala, are we sure it's okay for me to go?" He knew what I was referring to, or rather *who* I was referring to. Given our situation, we made sure to communicate any potential issues we might have and that included him telling me about how he found out about the gala... and the plus one he was *shockingly* not initially permitted to have.

"If you think for two seconds that I would be going to any event without you next to me, think again. She's been spoken to, my father is looking forward to seeing you, and Carlisle is grateful to have somebody else there that isn't afraid to speak like a human being. I want you there, little minx. It's perfectly okay for you to go," he promised and dammit the tears were coming back.

"Well, we can't have Carlisle left hanging in dull conversations, now can we?" I managed to huff a laugh. I went ahead and locked everything up and made my way back upstairs. Our take out would be arriving shortly and I was suddenly starving.

"No, we obviously can't," he said. *"I'm about to pull in, sweetheart. Are you still in the shop?"*

"No, I'm walking through the front door now. I'm ready for food, I forgot to bring snacks down with me and I absolutely regret that now."

"Bad, little minx! We'll get to that later, but for now I'm pulling in and it looks like our food is, too, so I'll feed your spoiled rotten ass in a minute," he fake fussed, then said, *"I love you!"* with a bunch of kissing noises before he ended the call.

This man, I swear.

Twenty-Four

Joshua

No matter what, I was determined to keep today a good day. Before the gala, I was able to get the keys to the house and finalized the plans with our friends. Everything was in motion and required mostly nothing from me outside of direction moving forward. Which was good, because Ingrid had definitely caught on to me being up to something.

Damn me and my inability to reign in my excitement when working on surprises.

Hell, I still didn't know how I managed to not act suspicious for our Christmas presents, but then again that may have been because, well, it was Christmas.

Ingrid and I were walking into the *Wild Haven* gala my mom set up. It must have been a newer venture of hers, as I couldn't remember her ever bringing it up. I usually liked to do research into the charities before attending, but I didn't have time with everything going on so I would have to learn as the evening progressed. When I looked down at Ingrid at my side on the carpet leading in, though, I didn't really care too much.

She was absolutely stunning. Not unlike other evenings, but I swore the more I was in her company, the more I realized just how truly *beautiful* she was.

Even with it being a red carpet event, she didn't go heavy handed on her make up, showcasing the freckles dotted across her cheeks and nose. She had her hair up in a slicked updo to showcase the neckline of her dress.

Fuck me, this dress.

I knew whatever she ended up wearing would give me a heart attack, but nothing could've prepared me for the plum, long sleeve gown she had on. The neckline in the front cut straight across her collar bones, while the back cut down into a low V that ended right below the middle of her spine. She paired it with this back necklace type thing that laid perfectly between her shoulder blades with small stones sparkling throughout. The front of the dress was just as beautiful, even if it was more subtle. The material hugged her curves impeccably as it draped down to the floor.

The best part of all, though? There was absolutely nothing underneath any of it. She said it was because of "lines," or whatever, but I liked to think it was a special treat just for me.

After getting through the carpet, photographs, and entry, we were finally escorted over to our table. I could see that they did well with making sure to place Carlisle and his date on the other side of Ingrid with my parents across from us.

"Who is Carlisle bringing?" Ingrid asked as I pulled the chair out for her to sit down.

I took a look at the name on the place setting next to his and saw *Bethany Carson* written in golden script. The name rang a bell but I couldn't put a face to it. "Someone named Bethany from the looks of it. I'm not sure who she is."

"She was assigned to me," Carlisle said as he appeared at the table next to Ingrid. "Your *mother* felt it necessary to give me a date since I didn't have one on my own. Ingrid, you know I love you, but now I think Quinn's matchmaking attention is on me."

Ingrid laughed as she shrugged her shoulders unapologetically. "I'd say I was sorry, but we both know I'm not."

Right as I was about to take my seat, I heard my mother approach me. I turned and saw that she was arm and arm with a taller blonde woman.

"Josh, dear, you made it! Have you met Bethany yet?" Out of the corner of my eye, I saw Ingrid straighten her spine and stand from her seat to move toward my side.

"I have not," I responded and then gave my attention to Bethany as I looped an arm around Ingrid's waist. "You're here with Carlisle this evening, correct?"

"I am, though I'm not sure where he went," she said with a bit of confusion. I looked around and saw that Carlisle had, in fact, fled the scene. I did my best to disguise my laugh as a cough before directing my eyes to my girl.

"Bethany, this is my girlfriend, Ingrid." I gestured toward her with one hand as I introduced them.

Mom seemed to have just noticed her, and her face went from sly excitement to disgust before she quickly schooled her features while she looked Ingrid up and down. "Oh. Ingrid, I didn't know you would be attending."

"Of course, Quinn. You know, I actually partner with *Wild Haven* from time to time and auction off vegan gowns," she said lightly, though I didn't miss the way my mom's face pricked with annoyance. I wasn't aware that Ingrid partnered with this charity, but I wasn't surprised.

"Wait, are you *the* Ingrid Morgan?" Bethany asked, looking like she was on the brink of fangirling. "I've been dreaming of the dress you did in the fall with the draped sleeves!"

"I am! Feel free to reach out if you're ever needing a gown. I have non-bridal related dresses as well." I could see it in Ingrid's face how excited she was and pride bloomed in my chest for her. She should be excited, I would genuinely never get over her talent.

Bethany and Ingrid walked away, arms linked together, to discuss more fashion, and I took the opportunity to speak with my mother more directly.

Before I could even open my mouth on the topic, she beat me to it. "I don't know what it is you see in her." She tsked her tongue. "You know, she doesn't plan on stopping her business to take care of the home?"

"Why should she? You do realize she is one of the most successful wedding dress designers in the state, right?" I couldn't for the life of me understand what her issue was with Ingrid but I was over her acting like this.

My mother just scoffed, like Ingrid's success didn't matter. "You know what it takes to be a part of this family, how much the women must do. At the very least, how they need to *look*."

Finally, it clicked. I stumbled back as though she had physically attacked me before straightening my spine and squaring my shoulders.

How *dare* she? How dare she speak about Ingrid like that?

"What is it that they should look like, *mother*? Should they not be beautiful both inside and out? Should they not have such a kindness in their heart, almost to a fault at times, putting others' needs above their own? Tell me, how should my future wife and mother of my children *look*?" I knew she could sense the fury in my tone just as much I could see the determination in her eyes, proving she wouldn't back down.

"She should at least be taking better care of herself and her presentation. That *girl* leaves nothing to the imagination in anything she wears with her clothes being so tight. It's unflattering and frankly, would be an embarrassment on the Astor name." She was doing her best to keep her composure, but her volume was getting louder as she barreled on and a crowd had started to form. "What will the public think with *that* hanging on your arm in pictures? What will they think of our family to see our *standards* stoop so low?"

I was almost positive I cracked a tooth from how hard I was clenching my jaw. "I don't necessarily care what they think. Ingrid is gorgeous, intelligent, and easily the most confident woman I've ever met. I'm so disappointed in you, Mother. How you live with this bigotry in your soul, I will never understand." I was *seething*. I'm not one to lose my temper, but this was by far some of the most asinine bullshit I've ever listened to.

Wait a fucking second...

"Did you have Carlisle bring Bethany to try to push her onto me? She's who you were trying to set me up with last month, isn't she?"

Instead of looking surprised, her face grew into a conspiratorial grin. Somehow, she still hadn't noticed the crowd growing around us, the murmurs whispering across the room as they watched with growing interest and the flash of cameras as they started recording. Maybe she just didn't care. I knew I didn't.

"So what if I did? Maybe I made sure he brought her so that you could see there are better options out there," she admitted, arms crossed over her chest.

Before I could get out another response, a small hand was placed on my arm just as my father approached my mother. I ignored him as I turned to see the hurt shining in Ingrid's eyes, the tears threatening to spill. I placed a kiss on the top of her head in apology and comfort.

I am so sorry, little minx.

"What the hell are you doing?" I heard my father hiss, just quiet enough for only the four of us to hear. "It's time for us to leave since you clearly can't control your tongue."

"We can't leave, I'm running this event. If anybody should be leaving, it's *her*. I specifically did not include her on the invite list, nor do I remember *allowing* you a plus one, Joshua," my mother announced, loud enough for the crowd to hear, proving that she *did* notice them.

I could hear Ingrid's quick inhale of breath as she squeezed my arm a little tighter. Then, like the strong queen she was, she faced off with my mother with the amount of grace Quinn *wished* she could pull off. "I was so excited to meet you, Quinn. I was so excited to potentially have a mother figure in my life after going the entirety of it without one. I see now that was a frivolous dream. I see now that I won't be good enough for you, but I'm more than enough for him. Excuse me."

With that, she walked away from me and the crowd parted itself to allow her a graceful exit. I took my eyes off of her and turned back to my mother one last time. "You should be ashamed of yourself. Don't expect an invitation to the wedding if that beautiful girl finds me worthy enough to spend the rest of her life with."

I turned on my heel and caught Carlisle's eye as he pointed in the direction I assumed Ingrid went. I chased after her, hoping my mother didn't just ruin all chances of a future I hoped to have with her.

Twenty-Five

Ingrid

*D*on't cry. Hold it in. If you trip and fall because you're too blind to see, you will never forgive yourself for the less than graceful dramatic exit.

"Ingrid!" Carlisle jogged up to my side, out of breath from chasing after me. "Where are you going?"

"I'm leaving. Do you know a way out of here other than back out on the carpet?" I knew enough about these events to know that the press was still out there, just hoping for a morsel of drama to unfold at any moment.

He frowned at me but then pointed in the direction of a hallway. "Follow this until you get to the exit sign. It'll take you to the back lot. I'll let Josh know where you're headed."

I nodded in thanks before grabbing my dress to hike it over my feet, and then I took off. Thankfully, I managed to grab my purse once I noticed what was happening. I sent Josh a text to tell him I was going to get a rideshare back to the island, and let him know to stay and try to enjoy himself.

I needed time to think. I needed time to breathe.

Luckily, given the event, a few rideshares were already waiting at the back entrance just in case anybody needed one before the night was over. I hopped in the first one and spouted off the address just as I saw Josh running out the back door. He yelled my name, but the car took off before I could even roll the window down to respond. In my purse, I could hear my phone ring and I took a shallow breath as I dug it out.

"Ingrid, baby, what are you doing?" he asked, out of breath, the moment I answered.

"I'm headed home," I said shakily. I could only keep the tears at bay for so long and I could feel them wavering the more I spoke. "Stay, enjoy the gala. I'm going to see if I can stay with one of the girls tonight. I just need some time to think and breathe."

"And you need to do this away from me?" I could hear the hurt in his voice, and as much as it pained me too, I had to do what I needed in order to take care of myself in this.

"I do. I'm sorry, Josh. I love you." As I hung up, I could hear him trying to keep me on the line, but I needed to message the girls and breathe.

SOS. Can I stay with one of you tonight?

Desi

I'm not home but I'll head there now. What's going on?

Char

I'm home and closer. Desi, grab her a bag from her place and meet us here. Wine or tequila?

Leave it to Char to go into immediate problem solving mode.

Tequila. No salt or lime. On my way now.

Desi

Fuck. Okay, I'm almost at your place now.

I gave the driver the updated address and leaned my head against the window. It wasn't Josh's fault and I knew that. I wasn't mad at him in the slightest, if anything hearing him come to my defence so quickly made my heart sing and break at the same time. I didn't even really care about what she said about me, but the fact that she so publicly felt it necessary to voice her issues and tried to set him up with somebody else in front of me was insulting on a multitude of levels.

Wild Haven would undoubtedly never conduct business with me again after that display. I could already hear the tabloids comments on "the fat girl on Joshua Astor III's arm". She didn't just humiliate me, she tried to come after my character and reputation. This could fall back on my father. *Oh god*, I internally groaned at the thought.

Could I marry into this family? I loved Josh so much but was it worth it? Could I spend the rest of my life worried about how she could potentially hurt the people I cared for at any given moment?

My phone was buzzing nonstop as Josh continued to try to get a hold of me before I inevitably just shut it off. I hated doing this to him, but if I tried to think everything through in his presence and company, I would just ignore the problem and not really consider the potential best answer.

The answer that resulted in no more *us*.

The car pulled up to Char's house and through the glass I could see both of them sitting on the porch as they waited for me, a bottle of tequila placed on the railing.

"What did he do?" Char instantly demanded. She was pissed but she was also worried. This wasn't like me. I didn't call the SOS signal.

I sighed as I took my heels off and grabbed the bottle before I headed toward the front door. "Tequila first, then I'll tell you." They opened the door for me as I uncorked the bottle with my teeth, spitting it onto the floor and downed the first shot.

"So, let me make sure I'm understanding," Desi began once I finished explaining everything as I drank half the bottle. "She made Carlisle bring a random woman with him as his date to try to set her up with Josh, talked shit about you not wanting to give up your business, and then proceeded to trash your appearance. Loudly. Publicly. At a charity gala."

"Mhm," I mumbled as I downed yet another shot. It didn't burn anymore. I'd officially reached the point of numbness that I'd been hoping for.

"And Josh defended you and chased after you and is likely still blowing up your phone," Char said as she reached for her own phone. It wasn't a question, we already knew the answers.

"Yep," I said, drunkenly popping the p.

"And you're here, getting drunk with us all mope instead of fucking him ten ways to Sunday because," Char continued with a wave of her hand.

"Because I need to not be in his presence right now. If I went home with him, I'd be doing exactly that instead of actually thinking anything through."

"What is there to think through?" Desi asked, gently and genuinely curious. They hadn't drunk nearly enough and it wasn't fair.

"Can I really marry into this family?" I choked up as I asked the one question I was the most scared to answer. My eyes were no longer trying to hold back the tears as they flowed messily down my face. Even if the answer was no, could I really leave him? After everything?

"Do you love him?" Char asked.

"You know I do. He's incredible. Also, have you *seen* him?!"

They both cackled before Desi leaned over and wrapped her arm around me so that I was curled into a ball at her side, my head on her shoulder. She grabbed a tissue from... somewhere. Char probably. She used it to wipe my tears away for me and I tried to swat her away.

"You two can tackle this together, as a team," she told me as though it was really that simple. Distantly, I heard a light knocking of some kind but ignored it. "I know how much he loves you, I can see it. Do you know how you two look at each other?" I stared up at her and shook my head as Char left the room mumbling something under her breath. "You look at each other like your parents did on their wedding day."

I inhaled quickly, more tears falling, as her words hit me square in the chest. I opened my mouth to respond but she cut off my efforts. "The love you two have is so strong it fills every room you enter together. Trust in him, have faith in your relationship, your partnership. Don't lose this because of her, then she wins."

I didn't know how to respond, so instead, I just nodded my head. Maybe it was that simple. Maybe just loving him and letting him love me really could fix this. Maybe that's all we really needed.

I heard the front door open and close in the entryway and two sets of footsteps headed our way as I turned to see who came over.

"Little minx?"

And there he was. My beautiful, most kind hearted, brilliant man.

Twenty-Six

Joshua

I 'd been losing my mind since the moment I saw Ingrid get into that car. My brain hadn't stopped spinning with thoughts ranging from concern for her, worry about our relationship, and pure vitriol for my mother.

She ruined everything. She hurt her. Ingrid left, she left and I don't know if she will even come back.

Carlisle found me outside the gala sitting on the ground with my back to the wall and my head in my hands. He managed to get my car from the valet and loaded me into the passenger seat. When I told him what happened, he didn't take me back to Ingrid's. Instead, he brought me to the penthouse, where we sat drinking scotch and brainstormed the next move.

"Maybe she just needs time, brother," he said simply as he took the smallest sip I had ever seen of his drink.

"She said that, but what if time ends up leading her to the decision that this isn't what she wants anymore? That *I'm* not what she wants anymore?" *Oh fuck, I won't survive this if I lose her for good.* I already felt like I was on the brink of a heart attack.

"She won't." He sounded so sure. Like this was a certain fact that couldn't be disputed. How could he possibly know for sure?

"I don't know what to do," I said, running my hands through my hair and abandoning my drink entirely. I didn't have the energy for liquor anymore. "How do I fix this?"

"You need to give her what she's asking for right now. Past that, it'll work itself out. Just give her what she needs." He was twirling the ice in his glass as his eyes glazed over, lost in thought.

"When did you get to be so wise about this shit?" I asked, but before he could respond, my phone pinged for the first time since Ingrid hung up on me.

Charlotte

Come over here and get your girl before she drinks herself into oblivion.

Fuck. If I knew my girl, I knew she was at least half a bottle of tequila deep and I didn't even think about how she might be coping, just that I knew she was in safe hands. But why was Charlotte asking me to come get her when she clearly asked for space?

I don't think she wants to see me right now...

Charlotte

I'm not even going to respond to that, just get over here and trust me.

She dropped a pin to give me her address and I looked up at Carlisle in pure shock. "Charlotte just texted me to come get Ingrid."

"Then what are you doing here with me? Go. I'll stay here tonight and get my car from the gala in the morning."

I didn't even change, just grabbed my keys and went. Thank *fuck* I didn't end up drinking more than half a glass.

I didn't give myself time to admire Charlotte's house before I raced up the stairs on her porch and forced myself to lightly knock on the door. I heard music playing and could see Charlotte's silhouette in the window as she opened it.

"Desi is in there working her magic right now," she said with a nod of her head. "I'm proud of you for how you handled it tonight. No garden shears for you. Now get her out of my house before she drinks all of my booze."

I gave her a firm nod and followed her into the living room where I could see Ingrid curled into Desiree's side. At the sound of my footsteps, she turned her head to look at me and the look on her face broke my heart into a million little pieces. She had the glassy eyed look from who even knew how many drinks and her skin was splotchy from crying. She'd changed into baggy sweats and an oversized sweater and I hated thinking that my mother's words made her feel uncomfortable in her own skin. I only hoped this was purely a choice for comfort and not an attempt to make herself feel smaller.

"Little minx?" I asked hesitantly, nervous to approach since the look on her face told me she definitely didn't know I was coming.

Shit, this isn't what she wanted. She asked for space. She doesn't want me here, doesn't want me—

My spiraling stilled the moment she lifted her arms and let out a broken sob as she cried my name. Instantly, I pulled her into my arms, her legs wrapping around my waist as she buried her head into the crook of my neck. She smelled like liquor and heart break but underneath it, I could still get the notes of her lavender espresso and I breathed her in just to confirm she was really letting me hold her.

"Oh sweet girl, come on. Let's go home." I squeezed her to me as she nodded her head absently and I saw Desiree unfolding herself to stand. She walked over to us and gave me a soft smile.

"It's going to be okay, Josh."

I carried Ingrid out to the car and placed her gently into the passenger seat. She seemed to have fallen asleep during the short journey and I brushed the hair off of her face as I put her seatbelt on. It was a short drive back to her apartment, but even still I had to force myself to look away from her and focus on the road the whole way there.

Once we made it home, I carefully carried her inside and placed her on the bed. Thankfully, it looked like she managed to take her makeup off at Charlotte's, likely per the girls' demands, so I didn't need to worry too much about that. I placed a glass of water and some pain reliever on the nightstand before I went into the closet to change out of my suit.

When I made it back over to the bed, I was suddenly struck with the realization she may not have wanted me in there. I inwardly groaned before bending down to place a kiss on her forehead and turned to resign myself to the couch for the night. Before I could take a step away from her, though, she managed to grab ahold of my hand.

"Stay," she pleaded in a soft, broken voice.

My heart ached as I climbed into my side of the bed and brought her into my arms. She curled into my chest and I could feel more tears landing on my skin as she silently cried.

"Shh, sweet girl," I soothed, running a hand over her back. "I'm not going anywhere. I'm right here." I kissed the crown of her head and held her tight while I let her feel what she was needing to.

Eventually, she drifted off and I felt her heart rate slow as her breathing evened out. I didn't sleep. Instead, I just continued to hold her and tried to formulate plans on how I was going to fix the mess my mother created.

I knew one thing for certain. I would never put Ingrid in a position like this ever again. I would never make her go through this kind of pain, so long as I could help it.

Twenty-Seven

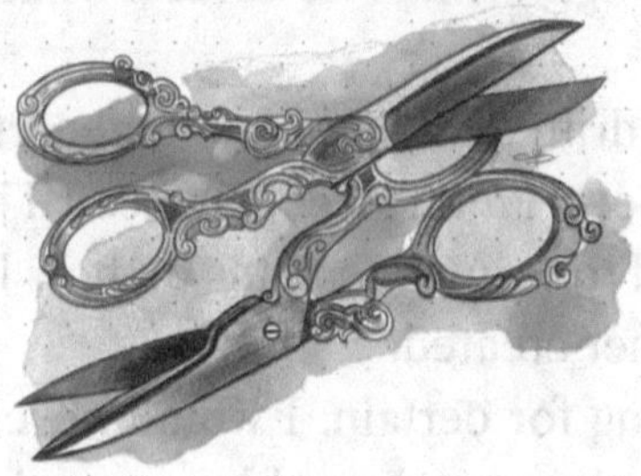

Ingrid

The moment my eyes opened, I couldn't take even two seconds to appreciate the warm embrace I was encapsulated in. With a panicked rush, I threw Josh's arm off of me and sprinted to the bathroom.

Of course, I tripped over the blanket that was caught around one foot, a shoe that was haphazardly on the floor in the hallway, and seemingly *air* right as I entered the bathroom, but I *did* manage to make it in time to throw the lid up and hurl what felt like an entire bottle of tequila into the toilet.

Fuck, I am never drinking again, I thought to myself as I felt his presence burst into the small bathroom behind me.

"Oh, sweetheart..." He dropped to his knees next to me and pulled my hair up to keep it out of my way. I wasn't doing a good enough job of it myself, if I was being honest.

178

He continued to rub soft circles in between my shoulder blades in a soothing gesture as I reached up to flush the evidence of why my liver will inevitably give out down the drain. Once I was sure I was done, I fell back onto my heels and leaned up against the side of the tub. Josh made quick work of getting my toothbrush ready for me before passing it over so I could remove the lingering taste from my mouth.

"Feelin' any better?" He grabbed the toothbrush back from me while I lazily spit into the toilet before flushing it one more time.

"Nope. I feel like I have been run over by an 18-wheeler and the only cure is a signature Joshua Astor the Third breakfast special." I needed greasy bacon, pancakes, and coffee as soon as humanly possible.

He hummed in agreement while scrunching his nose like he smelled something bad. "You need a shower first, little minx, then I will make you breakfast. How does that sound?"

He didn't even give me a chance to respond, just picked me up from the floor while I gave a small laugh before immediately wincing from the pain it caused behind my eyes. He reached behind me to turn on the shower before helping me get out of my clothes and his own. Once we were both disrobed, he got me into the shower.

Neither of us discussed the events of the night before while he methodically washed my entire body or when he lathered the shampoo through my long strands. We both seemed content to just let the conversation wait until we felt a little more human than either of us did at that moment.

I knew time was running out, though, when we were both dried and clothed in the kitchen.

I did my best to keep myself busy by working on our coffee, but when he saw me cringing away from the coffee grinder and espresso machine, he nudged me over to the island seating instead.

"I did some thinking last night," he began as he brought my mug filled with a lavender vanilla latte over to me. It took a little bit of time for him to get the ratios just right for my favorite caffeinated beverage, but I loved that he was persistent in figuring it out just so that he could make it for me. "I won't allow you to be put in a position like that again."

As important as this was, I really didn't want to talk about it. I held my head in my hands as I rubbed my temples in hopes that it would give me the strength I needed to participate in this discussion. "There isn't really a lot we can do about it, though. She's your mother at the end of the day. Short of going no contact with her, I really don't see how we would be able to stop something like last night from happening again."

He stilled at my words and gave me a pointed, determined look. He wasn't denying what I was saying.

No, I thought, *He surely doesn't plan to do that.*

"Ingrid..." Apparently he was.

"Josh, no! She's your mother! I can't expect you to just cut her out. Not to mention, going no contact with her would mean going no contact with your father, too." I shook my head, ignoring the pain that was starting to radiate down the length of my neck.

"If that's what needs to be done, then it will be done." The unyielding and firm look in his eye told me he wasn't kidding. He would really cut out his parents if it meant we could avoid a repeat of the night before. "Besides, I don't think it will come to that with my father."

Initially, I was shocked by that admission, but the more I considered him, I understood the truth behind it. Junior hadn't seemed too pleased with his wife at the gala and had attempted to get her to stop.

"Josh, if you are wanting to go no contact with your mother, I will support you regardless." I caught his eye as he started looking away and waited until I knew his attention was solely on me. "But, I don't want you to make this decision, one so large and potentially detrimental to your family, purely just because of me. If this is what you are wanting to do, then I need you to make sure this is something that *you* are wanting."

"Ingrid, you are my family," he started and before I could even begin to formulate a response, he continued. "Maybe I haven't made myself clear? Ingrid we are looking at buying a home together. To share and to grow our lives in. We have been planning a future together. So if I need to remove some toxicity from *our* lives, then that is what I will do. I'm not going to sit back and allow somebody to attack my family, even if the attack is coming from family themselves."

I didn't know how to respond to that. Obviously, he was right, we were doing all of those things. We were trying to plant the seeds that would grow into the rest of our lives. I knew that, I did, but I didn't anticipate him considering me family already. I mean, in the legal sense, I was just another person that he happened to be living with. A roommate. Somebody who eats the food he cooked.

"I'm family to you?" I asked, hesitantly, both in hope and uncertainty.

He seemed to catch on those emotions immediately because he said, "Of course you are, little minx. You're the only family that truly matters, because you are the future. *My* future."

I didn't know if it was the words he said, the lingering hangover, or the exhaustion that made me burst into tears. It had likely been a culmination of all three.

"Baby..."

Josh met me at the barstool before I could even fully remove myself and dragged me into his arms. "Sweetheart, did you really not think that's what this was? Do you not realize who you are to me?"

I was getting tears and snot all over his bare chest, but he didn't seem to mind. He just wrapped his arms tight around me and waited until I was calm enough to answer him.

"I haven't really been anybody's family before." I was hiccupping as I tried to get the words out. "I know I have my dad and the girls, but outside of them I've never planned for a future with anybody before. I never expected anybody to want me as their family."

He tutted his tongue before grabbing me by the thighs and hoisting me up onto the island. He grasped my chin between his thumb and forefinger, ensuring that I couldn't look away from him even if I tried. "You're right, I don't *want* you as my family, Ingrid. I *need* you as my family. So, I am going to go no contact with Quinn. I will speak with my father and ensure the two of us are on the same page. I won't allow this to cause any further issue and I sure as hell won't allow her to continue to hurt the woman I love. The woman I plan to spend the rest of my life with."

I didn't know what to say in response to that. I didn't know what I could even possibly say to him at that moment.

He needed *me as his family*.

"Now..." I watched as the man I could have never imagined finding dropped his hand from my chin to tap me on the nose before he let his fingers fall naturally on my bare thighs, trailing gentle strokes up and down them. "I believe you are still owed breakfast, my love. So what will it be today? Waffles or pancakes?"

Twenty-Eight

Joshua

"Dad. You got a minute?"

I wasted no time in setting my plan into motion. After Ingrid and I's conversation over the weekend about what I was hoping to do, I knew this issue would need to be settled immediately. If I never had to deal with another night like the evening of the gala, it would be a night too soon.

I spent a decent amount of time on Sunday getting meetings set up and checking over schedules to ensure I would be able to do what needed done.

Which was how I wound up at my fathers office door, interrupting his mid day "stare into the abyss that is a computer screen while actually not getting anything done" time.

At the sound of my voice, he looked up and gave a hefty sigh. "I do. I take it you have an explanation for the meeting that appeared on my calendar this morning?"

Ah yes, the meeting. I hadn't been kidding when I said I had been busy. "Among other things."

He studied me for a moment. He should've been more than aware of what I was needing to talk about. He was there the night of the gala, he heard what my mother, *his wife*, had been spewing. I knew he wasn't happy about it, but even with all of the reassurances I gave Ingrid, there was still a portion of doubt that I held.

It didn't matter, though. If my father decided that he would side with Quinn, then I would do what needed to be done, even if it wasn't the route I planned.

"I noticed your mother was also added to the meeting, is this about the gala?" The fact that he assumed correctly gave me a spark of hope. He hadn't assumed that I would be informing her of my plans with Ingrid or our relationship, not that I would be doing that anyways, but it reinforced the notion that I wouldn't need to lose him as well.

I nodded to him in confirmation before I said, "I came by to give you a heads up of what my course of action is here. Please understand that my decision is made."

"Son, please just tell me, the dramatics aren't really necessary."

"Well, excuse me for wanting to feel like a super hero, here to save the day so well that I get the girl in the end." Our shared laughter was strained. We both knew the seriousness of the matter. "I'm going no contact with Quinn. She will not be invited to the wedding, and I will not be attending any family functions that include her."

He didn't look surprised, more defeated. He looked as though how I handled this would determine his own course of action. "What will this mean for you and I? The company isn't a concern, you earned your spot and your inevitable promotion, but what about the holidays? Would I still be invited to your own events?"

"We have some time to figure out the plan for the holidays, but so long as you aren't directly taking her side and cutting me off, this won't change anything between you and I. You would still be invited to everything, you just won't be granted a plus one."

He nodded in a way that told me he understood the boundaries I was laying at his feet. "You really love this girl, don't you?"

"I do. She's my family. Even if she wasn't, I have zero desire to associate myself with somebody that acted the way my own mother did at the gala." I watched him carefully to gauge his emotions. He wasn't holding them too close to his face but I couldn't help the anxious energy brewing in me. There was no chance in hell that I would be backing out on this plan, but I really didn't want to have to lose my father in the process of this.

"I tried to discuss her behavior with her over the weekend," he said so quietly I almost didn't hear him. He had turned his head down to look at his hands and I could see that he was spinning his wedding band as he worked through his thoughts. "She wouldn't even humor it. She just brushed it off like it wasn't a big deal. I'm not surprised by your reaction to this, son, and I'm not going to ask you to reconsider your decision. If I were in your position, I would do the same thing. You have my support in this."

He sounded so tired. I wasn't sure how he would handle this on his own end, but I knew that I would give him my own support in turn should he need it. "I appreciate it, dad. I didn't want it to come to this, but honestly, hearing you say that just secured this decision for me."

We moved on to shop talk to distract ourselves from the meeting to come. We both had relatively slow days, which I personally took as a welcome gift from the universe, so we were able to stay in his office and actually spend some time together. Even though we worked with each other we didn't always get to have this, as our schedules rarely lined up well enough to allow it. Far be it from me to spend the entirety of our time together just harping on what was to come.

I told him about Ingrid and even invited him to the surprise I had planned out for the end of February. He, of course, was excited as this meant he would have the opportunity to meet Senator Morgan. Apparently he had a few legislation ideas he was wanting to run by him. I was pretty sure he just wanted to say he got to not only meet the beloved Senator, but that said Senator would be joining his family, but what did I know?

My watch pinged to let me know that it was time for the meeting at the same time his own did. We both sighed and made eye contact before he said, "Let's get this over with, shall we?"

My mother was already sitting at the conference table when my dad and I entered the room. She looked completely stress free if not just mildly annoyed for having to leave what I was sure was a very busy day of... whatever it was my mother did all day. I really wasn't sure. I didn't really know what to make of her blasé attitude, other than the fact that it filled me with a type of quiet rage I wasn't used to feeling.

She finally looked up and I watched as she put on the pleasant mask that she always wore. "This was such a surprise to see on my calendar this morning," she said as she moved across the room to give us both a hug. I didn't hug her back. In fact, it took every ounce of my strength to not just push her away entirely.

She really just thought everything was fine. How had I never noticed how fucking delusional my mother was?

"Go ahead and take a seat, Quinn. Our son would like to discuss some things with you."

She arched an eyebrow in challenge but complied and sat back in her seat. I tried not to smile at the way my father made a point to sit next to me across the table from her instead of at her side.

"Do you have an explanation for what happened at the gala?" I wasn't wasting time thanking her for coming, I was beyond pleasantries at this point.

With her head cocked to the side in mock confusion she said, "I'm not sure what you mean, Joshua."

"Quinn, don't."

"What? I truly don't know what he means." She looked over at me, the challenge still gleaming in her eyes. "Are you referring to how your little girlfriend stormed out of my event, causing a scene?"

I looked at my father, genuine shock covering my features. I noticed there was no surprise on his own face and at first I was confused by that until I remembered that he had already tried to have this conversation with her. He just looked utterly exhausted.

I cleared my throat to help gather my thoughts. "Close, mother, but not quite." She opened her mouth to say something, but I raised a hand to cut her off. "No, you will allow me to say what needs to be said. I called this meeting, after all. I set the agenda." I waited for her to nod before I continued. "I am doing you the courtesy of having this conversation instead of simply taking action first. I was hoping that you would, at bare minimum, have or show any kind of remorse for the way you treated and spoke about Ingrid, but seeing as you don't then I won't bother going over it again with you. From this moment forth, you and I will have no contact with one another. I will no longer be attending any of your events, including holidays. I told you at the gala that if Ingrid ever allowed me the privilege of marrying her that you would be lucky to receive an invitation. After further consideration, I have determined you are not even worthy of that.

"I don't know what came over you at the gala, I don't know when you became such a vile woman, but I have zero desire to allow you to continue to infect my life and my family with your poison. Ingrid was *so* excited to meet you and you have been nothing but hurtful toward her since the day you met her. Because no, I haven't forgotten what you said to her at the Christmas party. She was nothing but kind despite the fact that you didn't deserve it."

She scoffed at me and said, "You don't mean this, you know as well as I do that you and her won't last. She isn't family material. Not *Astor* family, anyways. I was just saying what everybody else was too afraid to say."

"No, Quinn, you weren't." I was grateful to have my father back me up, I didn't want him to fight my battles for me, but at that point, I didn't have it in me to stop him. "Ingrid is a lovely girl. You couldn't have picked a better match for him if you tried, which if memory serves me right, you did. Instead of just being happy that our son found love, you chose to be hurtful to not just her but to him, as well. *That* isn't a trait worthy of the Astor family."

I did my best not to read too much into what he said. The implications were clear, but how he chose to handle the situation with my mother was his decision and I didn't need to try to get into the middle of it. Regardless, those same implications seemed to be the only thing that made her genuinely take pause.

My mother, simply put, was just another gold digger. What an unfortunate realization to have.

I watched as she tried to come up with some excuse, some way to justify herself or some other form of non-apology to give. I didn't want to hear it. Instead, I simply stood up and buttoned my suit jacket and said, "That's all I have for you. I have already begun measures to have you removed from my life." I then turned to my father. "I am going to take the rest of my work home today."

I left the two of them to discuss, what I could only assume, their own marital issues. With all of this out of the way, I could finally put my focus back into my surprise for Ingrid.

I just hoped that there were no other hiccups along the way.

Twenty-Nine

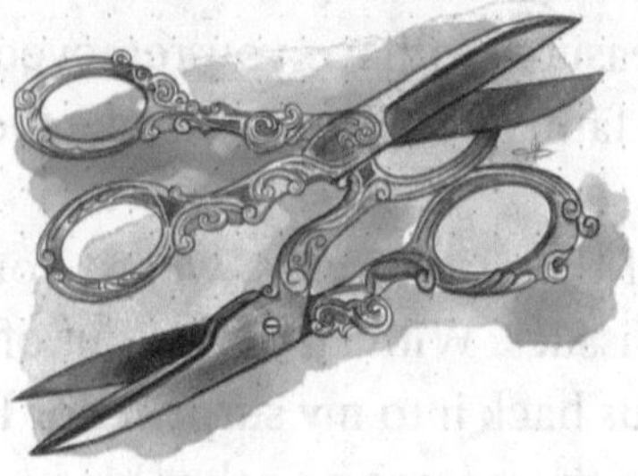

Ingrid

I was working on sewing the second dress in my spring collection when I heard the bell above my shop door chime.

"Checking for signs of life!" I turned just in time to see Char and Desi storming in with a pastry bag and coffee, hopefully to share.

"I'm alive I swear, the taffeta hasn't gotten me yet!" They both gave me a skeptical look, lifted brow and all, and when I looked down at the scene around me I realized I was indeed submerged in taffeta. "Okay, this looks bad. Help me up please."

"Ingrid, this is *stunning*, I want one like this when I get married one day," Desi said as she circled around the dress, ignoring my outstretched hand entirely to just admire the dress.

"You say that every time, Desi. At this point, the dress she makes you will just be a pile of fabric with a zipper sewed in."

Char, at least, grabbed my hand and helped me up while Desi attempted to look offended.

I chose to ignore their bickering behind me as I searched through the coffee and food they placed on my desk in the corner of the room. After I located my lavender latte and cream cheese danish, I tried to tune back into the conversation. It sounded like they were still bickering though, so it was easy for my mind to wander.

Making the dresses was a welcome distraction to everything going on, but with my hands idle, I couldn't stop the racing thoughts. Josh was finally back to being his normal self but it still felt like something was up with him. I couldn't tell if it was the lingering effects of his decision to cut off his mom a couple of weeks ago or if it was something else entirely, but it was making me nervous.

It was a big decision for him to decide to go no contact with her. From what he'd told me, it sounded like his dad was also making decisions in regards to her as well, and that just made me feel even more guilty than I already did. I didn't want to just *obliterate* an entire family. No matter how many times Josh assures me, I still felt awful.

"Earth to Ingrid!" Char was standing directly in front of me waving her hands across my face to gain my attention. I had to physically blink myself back into the conversation and my friends.

I rubbed a hand across my face, almost spilling my coffee in the process before Desi swooped in to grab it from my hand. "Ugh, I'm sorry. What's going on?"

"We were asking how you were doing with everything," Desi studied me for a moment before adding, "But I think that little space out answers that question for us."

I winced but didn't respond. She wasn't wrong, I really was having a hard time with everything and if it weren't for my work, I would be losing my damn mind.

"What's going on in that brain of yours?" Desi questioned with a concerned look on her face.

"Wait, don't answer! Let me guess." Char sounded way too excited to do exactly that, but I was simply out of energy to stop her. "She's thinking 'Oh no, Joshypoo cut off his wench of a mother because she was mean to me! It's all my fault! I'm a homewrecker!' Did I nail it?"

"Bitch," I muttered as I grabbed my latte back from Desi and took a sip.

"Oh, you're totally right," Desi said. "Ingrid, you do realize he is a grown ass man who can make his own choices, right?"

I rolled my eyes at her. "Of course, I know that. Doesn't change the fact that he quite literally no longer has a relationship with his mother because of me."

They both groaned very dramatically. "Ingrid, babe, it's not that simple and you know it isn't. If he is telling you that he is secure in his decision and that he doesn't regret it, you need to just believe him." Desi was, as always, the voice of reason.

"Not only that, but you literally didn't do anything except exist. It's not your fault that she was a bitch for the sake of being a bitch." And then there was Char, being the voice of, well, violence.

"Is it really just that simple though? His thoughts on it, I mean." I didn't realize how bad I needed the reassurance until then.

"Girl, he's a man," Char reasoned. "I promise, it really is that simple.

They were both looking at me with gentle reassurance. It was hard not to believe them when I understood what they were both telling me. Josh was acting weird prior to the gala so the issues with his mom couldn't have been the reason for his behavior two weeks later. Which begged the question...

"Okay, so if he really is as unbothered about his mother as you two seem to think he is, what the hell has been up with him lately? He's been acting shady since New Years."

Suddenly, everything in the room looked more interesting to the both of them as they took simultaneous sips of their own coffees and looked around at the boutique. "What the hell guys?"

"Hmm?" Desi swallowed a massive gulp of her coffee and pretended to focus back on me. "Oh, um, I don't know. I'm sure it's nothing."

"Yeah! Nothing at all! Ooo are these the sketches for the other dresses?"

"Wait a second, what do you two know?" They both turned to look at me and just stood there with shit eating grins.

"Nothing!" They said in unison. I narrowed my eyes at them both. They absolutely knew something. I would let them keep their secrets, though, because it seemed like whatever it was would be something I enjoyed. This also made me feel significantly better about whatever the hell was going on with Josh.

"Mhm, sure, whatever you say."

The girls helped me the rest of the day with working on the collection. We managed to finish the second dress as well as get through the bulk of the third, which I was eternally grateful for.

Right before the girls left, Desi pulled me aside to give me a hug and grabbed my face in both hands to make me look at her.

"Trust him, Ingrid. He loves you. *Let him.*"

"MINXY BABY!"

Oh god, this was how I would die.
"WAKE UP!"
Why was he being so loud? What was happening?
"LITTLE MINX!"
Oomph.

I opened my eyes to see Joshua Astor III's face directly in front of my own. He was smiling so big, and any annoyance I had at being awoken so aggressively immediately went right out of the window. He looked so cute, his hair was tousled like he had been up and moving around doing... *something*.

"Oh good! You're awake!" He looked so excited, he was still giving me a big goofy smile.

I gave him a small smile of my own and laughed as I said, "Well, you see, there was a man yelling for me. What is going on with you this morning?"

He leaned down and gave me a smattering of kisses all over my face, still looking overly joyful for whatever time it was.

"It's love day! Sit up, please I have sustenance for you." He didn't even give me two seconds to react to what he was telling me to do. He just lifted me up while somehow simultaneously fluffing the pillow behind my back. Without any warning at all, a tray, that I don't know where he got, appeared on my lap.

The first item to catch my eye was a plate of fluffy French toast with fresh strawberries and powdered sugar on top. Next to it was my favorite lavender fork along with my mug filled with my favorite latte. I noticed in the corner of the tray was a smaller vase filled with mini wildflower bouquet complete with sprigs of lavender.

"Love day?" I asked him with what I was sure were hearts in my eyes. "You'll have to enlighten me, as you see I just woke up and I don't even know what day it is."

"Well, little minx," he said with a boop to my nose. "Today is Friday, February 14th. Which means you aren't working today and I get to spoil you. I already rescheduled my entire day so that I could stay with you and before you argue that you have dresses to create, you have been working so hard these past couple of weeks and are back ahead of schedule and deserve a break. I am mildly over you coming in at the end of the day with more Band-Aids on your fingers from needle pricks."

He put on his faux stern face with me and I knew that if I told him that I couldn't afford to take a day off that he wouldn't force me to anyways, even if he ultimately believed I needed the break. Lucky for him, I was more than happy to take one as I was pretty sure I couldn't feel my fingertips anymore after the last round of sewing.

I picked up my fork and was about to start digging in when I noticed something.

"Wait, where's your breakfast? I don't want to eat without you."

He made an "ah" sound accompanied by lifting a finger in the air as if to say *one second, please*. He then bent down next to the foot of the bed and when he straightened himself back to his full height, he was holding a second tray with his own breakfast, minus the flowers. In the most careful manner I was sure he could muster, he climbed onto the bed next to me, tray still in hand, doing his best to make sure that he didn't spill anything. Once he was settled, he looked over at me with a smug grin.

"Better?" He teased.

All I could do was laugh and start working on the meal he made me. "I wish I had a camera recording for that. That took some real skill, Joshua Astor the Third."

"Oh, I think you will find that I am incredibly talented in a multitude of areas." A shiver ran down my spine as I remembered *exactly* how talented he was.

Judging by the look on his face as he licked his syrup coated fork, he knew exactly where my brain headed.

Oh, it was going to be a long *day.*

Thirty

Joshua

I spent the entire day spoiling her. Little did she know that the entire time me and her were out and about, the first leg of my surprise was taking place behind the scenes.

I kept doing my best to discretely respond to texts without her noticing, especially since I made such a big deal about today being all about her. I didn't want her to think for two seconds that I wasn't being present and in the moment with her.

It was hard though, especially when I was juggling my racing thoughts on the surprise and watching her lick her ice cream in the most seductive fucking manner I had ever seen.

Actually, I was only really focused on one thing.

She was saying something to me, I could hear the pretty lilt of her voice, but my focus was solely on a drop of lingering ice cream on the center of her lip. Each time I attempted to focus my attention back to what she was saying, my eyes would drift right back to that spot on her lip.

"Minxy baby, shh for just a second, please," I pleaded with her. I heard her make a noise of complaint, but I ignored it as I leaned in and wiped my thumb over the black cherry ice cream before I brought it to my own lip. I watched as her own eyes lingered on the movement while her tongue reached out to lick the spot my thumb just touched.

"Okay, I need you to start over what you were telling me, because I am so sorry to tell you, I was not listening."

"Bold of you to assume that I remember anything I was just saying, let alone my own name, after that performance, Josh." The look on her face told me everything I needed to know. I could have sworn I heard a small whimper escape from her when I leaned into her again, this time choosing to let my teeth graze over the line of her jaw.

I had taken her to Central Park, and while I made a comment that it may be too cold for ice cream outside, she had simply dismissed me with a wave of her hand and said something along the lines of "I'm not going to avoid my second favorite desert just because it's cold outside, Josh."

Okay, that was exactly what she said to me. When I asked what her *first* favorite was, she just gave me a wink and sauntered deeper into the park to locate a spot for us to relax.

Which was how we ended up on the park bench we were sitting on, and while I knew the cold wasn't helping, I gave myself a mental pat on the back at the shiver that ran through her when I dragged my mouth up and lightly sucked on the lobe of her ear.

"I think it's time for us to get somewhere warm, little minx, what do you think?" I kept my voice low in her ear before pulling back slightly to wait for her response.

She really did let out a full blown whine at that. "But, home is so far away."

Oh, little minx, you have no idea.

"What if I told you that I had a feeling we were going to want privacy sooner than when we got back?"

She raised both of her eyebrows but she couldn't stop the evil little grin that graced her features. "What did you do?"

"Oh, you know, nothing crazy. I just booked us a hotel room a couple of blocks away and already had a small overnight bag packed for the both of us and sent to our room." I was a genius. I was the smartest man to ever man. The look of just pure excitement on her face proved it.

"Well, what the fuck are we doing freezing our asses off on a park bench for?"

We didn't even make it to the room.

I had her scarf wrapped around my hand at reception, her beanie in my coat pocket in the elevator, and I was pretty sure the sleeve of my own coat was trapped in the hotel room door from her forcing it off of me while I tried unlocking it.

We couldn't even make it to the bed before I had her pinned against the wall with her legs wrapped around my hips. She was doing everything in her power to gain some friction where she needed it as she mindlessly grinded herself against me.

Between nips and sucks, she said, "Josh, please, I need you."

I believed her. If she needed me like I needed her, then it was like drowning in a pool of water and needing that gulp of air to stave off dying. I needed her like my life depended on it. Hell, at that point, I was pretty sure my life *did* depend on her.

Was that healthy? Probably not. But she tasted like my dreams coming true. She felt like my greatest accomplishment. I would be fucking *damned* if I lost this, lost *her*.

So, to ensure that never happened, I carried her over to the bed and dropped her onto the plush hotel duvets. She wouldn't stay laid out for me, almost immediately she sat up to work on the rest of her clothes, like she couldn't stand to have anything else touching her right now. Normally, I would play mad at that, but instead of giving her a reprimand, I stayed standing and worked on my own as I watched her.

"I wanted to try something today," I started as I moved around the room toward our overnight bag. I felt her eyes trail after me as I opened it up and retrieved the small bottle I was looking for as well as a condom. "Are you feeling adventurous?"

"With you? Always, Joshua. I trust you."

My back was to her, so she couldn't see completely how her words affected me, and for that I was grateful.

She trusted me.

I took a deep breath and stroked myself for the simple act of needing *something* to satiate the ache, if only temporarily. As I walked back over toward her, I watched as she took in the items I was holding. She arched an eyebrow at me in question.

"Go ahead, ask what you need to," I encouraged. I was never going to discourage her curiosity when we tried something new. If she needed clarification, I would always give it to her.

"I understand the lube, but why the condom?" She really was such a perfect woman for not shying away from me.

I climbed onto the bed and tapped the tip of her nose before crawling over her body to leave a trail of kisses. "Because, little minx, I don't plan on coming inside of your ass. There is only one place I want to finish inside of you, and as much as I know it will be difficult, your tight ass is not it. The condom, sweet girl, is so that I can keep you safe."

Her nails made it into my hair as I continued making my way down her body. I licked, sucked, kissed, and nipped at every single one of her dips and curves. I would never get over how absolutely perfect she was.

"Josh…"

"Shh, I know what you need." I spread her legs out for me to feast. "I need an informed answer from you before we begin, are you sure this alright with you?"

"Yes, Josh, please. I need you."

At her permission, I sat up and flipped her with ease onto her stomach. She let out a yelp as I lifted her up to her knees with one arm while holding her chest down with the opposite hand. She wiggled her ass into me as I dragged my fingertips over her skin teasingly. I leaned down so that I could draw patterns with my tongue up the backs of her thighs one at a time before moving north to bite her right cheek.

I couldn't go without tasting her if I tried, which I wasn't, so I caved and finally licked up her center.

Fuuuuuuck, I would never get over how delectable she was.

"I told you I would do this eventually. That I would claim and consume you in every possible way imaginable. Didn't I, minxy baby?" I didn't allow her a moment's reprieve to respond before my lips latched onto her clit and sucked into my mouth. I wanted to make sure she was relaxed for what I had planned, so with one hand spreading her wide to me, I inserted two fingers directly into her core to massage her g-spot.

When I leaned back to look at the masterpiece that she was, I watched her legs tremble and struggle to continue to hold her up. She was already so close to coming and I had barely gotten started.

"Don't hold it in, Ingrid. I want to hear you scream. If we don't get a noise complaint, I didn't do my job well enough." I removed my hand from inside of her to slap three quick swats directly onto her clit to help encourage her along.

It worked. Again, I was a genius.

She screamed and I sat back on my heels and watched as she clenched on absolutely nothing, the evidence of her orgasm dripping down her center and onto the comforter beneath her.

Yeah, there was no fucking way I wasn't recreating that with my own.

I reached to the side to grab the condom and lube from next to her. I ripped the wrapper open with my teeth, and the sound of that action alone was enough for her pussy to pulse and clench again in aftershock. Once I was covered, I flipped the cap open and coated two fingers before I let the cold liquid drip onto her puckered hole. She shivered at the feeling, letting out a small moan, and I almost came from the sound alone.

"I don't have you gagged today, which means I need you to use your words if this is too much for you. Do you have a word in mind that you would like to use?" While I waited, I gently massaged the lubricant into the ring of muscles.

"Ch-cherry," she stuttered.

I gave a small smile that she couldn't see as I pressed the tip of my finger into her. "Still have ice cream on the brain, sweetheart? Have I not distracted you enough?" She was past the point of forming words, so I took it easy on her when I could hear her struggle. "That's a perfect choice. Tell me one more time so that I know you know what to say if you need to stop."

"Cherry!"

I murmured gentle praise and rewarded her with a kiss to the base of her spine. She tensed up some as I breached the second knuckle on my index finger, and I did my best to soothe her and bring her back to her pliant state.

"Relax, minxy baby. You're doing so good. That's it, let me in." She slowly but surely relaxed more and more as my reassurance washed over her. I could visibly see the tension leaving her body as she melted further into the mattress. Let alone the fact that I could *feel* her lean into me more, her trust that she allowed me flowing from her own body to my own.

"Are you ready for another?" She made an incoherent noise in repose. "Words, Ingrid. I need you to use your words, otherwise this isn't going to work."

"Yes, p-please. More."

And who was I to deny her? I couldn't. I would never.

We slowly worked together to get her stretched as well as we could for her to be able to take me. Before either of us knew it, I was pouring more lube onto my sheathed cock and onto her.

"Alright, little minx, check in time." If she didn't say yes, I would have to leave the hotel room. No, I would have to leave the entire building. I felt as though I was going to explode. "Are you ready for me?"

She didn't need the encouragement that time. "More, Josh. I can take it."

Before she could tense back up and we lost the progress we made, I pressed just the tip of my dick inside of her. Of course, my little minx was eager as ever as she wiggled her ass onto me and tried pressing into me more. I had to hold onto her hips in a bruising grip to keep from letting her to avoid hurting her at all.

"You're doing so good, Ingrid." I wish I had a camera to capture how incredible she looked. I would hang this image in our bedroom. In my office. On the dashboard of my fucking car, I wanted this to be the only sight I saw until the day I fucking died.

With the most restraint I had ever held, I slowly pushed into her, stopping periodically to check in with her as I went. Once I settled all the way to the hilt, I halted my movements to gather my composure. If I wasn't careful, I would go off course and my inner plan would be ruined.

Well, it wouldn't be ruined, but I had zero desire to come in a fucking condom when it should buried deep inside of her instead.

"I want you to take over, baby, can you do that for me?" I genuinely couldn't trust myself at that point to not just rut into her. Of course, she was as eager as I had ever seen her and immediately started moving herself slowly up and down my length. I kept myself in check as I kept my grip on her firm while still allowing her to take full control.

"Good girl, take what you need from me. Let me fucking give you exactly what you're craving." Her moans were going to be the death of me. She always sounded so fucking pretty when she had herself impaled on my dick.

"Keep squeezing me. You're so close, aren't you?" If I thought her pussy was tight, nothing and I meant *nothing*, compared to the way her ass held onto me.

"Don't hold out on me, Ingrid. What did I say before? I want them all." She was getting closer and closer to her orgasm.

"*Now*."

The sound that came out of her as she finally reached her climax was nothing short of absolutely, devastatingly, *feral*. I gripped onto her hips and pushed her off of me to quickly rip the condom off and without wasting a single second, pushed directly into her completely soaked cunt. The moment for her to be in control was over. She spiraled into another orgasm before her second one even had a chance to finish consuming her and that was all it took for me to follow her lead.

I blacked out. I must have. She had a way of doing that to me where one moment, I was quite literally balls deep inside of her and the next moment I was trembling and unable to catch my own breath. I had her chest back to being buried into the bed as I fucked her through the aftershocks of both of our orgasms and when I finally pulled out, I kept her lifted up so I could watch.

I changed my mind. *That* was the image I wanted to see for the rest of my life. Burn a copy and add it to my urn, I never wanted to see anything else.

I knew I needed to get her cleaned up, but I couldn't help myself as I used a clean finger to catch my seed escaping her and pushed it back inside. One day, she would give me the privilege to put a little mini me or mini her inside of her and I found I wanted nothing more.

Once we were both cleaned up, I dragged her with me under the blankets and into my arms.

"Do you want breakfast here in the morning sweet girl?" She was all pliant and glowy and looking like the best gift I could ever have. I brushed some of the hair out of her eyes and just watched her as she snuggled further into me.

"We can, but I know it won't be as good as yours," she mumbled quietly into my chest. Before she fell asleep, she added, "Yours is the best breakfast."

Thirty-One

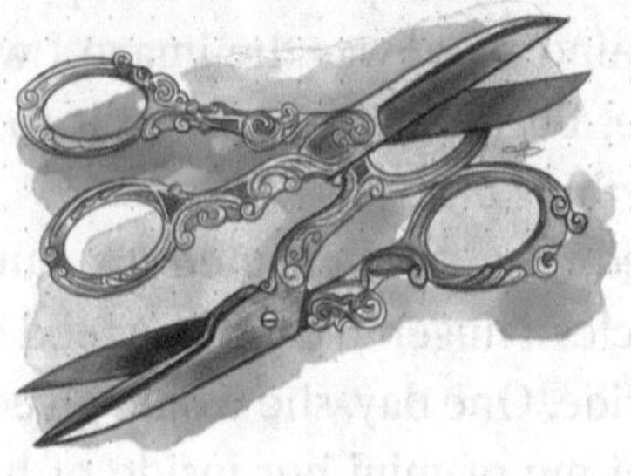

Ingrid

"**Y**ou're not going with that color are you?" Char asked next to me.

She sounded a little panicked, which almost made me laugh. The girls had decided to take me out to celebrate that I was officially finished with my spring collection, *Fly Away with Me*. I ended up using a lot of butterfly inspiration for the collection this year, and I couldn't think of a better way to describe it.

I blamed the flutters my own relationship caused, but I digressed.

"Wait, Ingrid. You can't do neon green. What is happening right now?" Desi sounded just as panicked as Char did and that time I *did* laugh, because of course I wasn't going to get neon green on my nails.

"Will you both chill? I was just looking at it." It had been forever since we did a spa day and I was so excited to just feel pampered for a little bit.

"Here, you should get this color." Desi handed me a bottle of a pretty baby pink gel polish. I shrugged and grabbed it. I wasn't picky and I trusted my girls to know what would work for me.

"So, you said Josh is taking you out for a late lunch after this?" Char asked from my right once we sat down next to one another in the salon chairs.

"Yeah, he said he had a meeting this evening and he wasn't able to get it rescheduled. Something about Tokyo time or whatever." I wished he was able to spend the evening with me without distraction. It felt like forever ago since our hotel getaway even though it had only been a couple of weeks.

Luckily, it was Friday, so I would get to have him the entire weekend before it was business as usual come Monday.

"Do we need to bring you back to your place after this or is he picking you up here?" Desi asked from my other side as she watched the nail artist get started on hers. She had chosen a deep blue for her own nails.

"He's picking me up from here and gave me explicit instructions that I am not to pay for my appointment today. I left with his black Amex and I'm pretty sure he even removed all forms of payment from my wallet just to make sure I didn't try to pay for my own gift."

Char snorted. "Of course he did. You're independent to a fault sometimes, girl."

I heard Desi hum in agreement as I turned and looked at Char, who was getting a chocolate brown on her nails. "I am not! And even if I was, could you blame me? I've been on my own since the moment I left for college."

"Yeah, but it's okay to let somebody take the reins every once in a while." I knew Desi meant in the life aspect sense, but I had to forcibly stop myself from reacting in all of the *other* ways I definitely had no qualms with Josh taking control.

I was still sore from the way he had me bound and gagged the night before.

Shaking off the burst of arousal that was flooding my veins, I focused back on the conversation at hand.

"I don't want to bring this up, because things seem really good right now between you two, but I feel like we are due for a check in." Any time Char decided to get serious, I knew I needed to give her my full attention. "Is his mother causing any more issues? Are we past all of that nonsense?"

I took my time in answering her. The first question was easy enough; no, she wasn't causing any issues at all. In fact it seemed like he was doing really well with everything. His relationship with his dad wasn't even strained like I had been worried about. Neither of us were really shocked to hear that Junior had filed for divorce. I was just glad that Quinn wouldn't be getting anything given how she disrespected both of them. It was the second question that I wanted to make sure I thought through before answering.

"I haven't heard of her attempting to reach out at all so I am trying this new thing where I simply trust him. Yes, we are past it. He seems good. We both are."

"Thank god, I didn't want to have to replace my good wire cutters. I would, but they're expensive and you got them for me." I wasn't sure how Desi had been internally planning to cause mayhem on Quinn with wire cutters, but I appreciated the sentiment regardless.

We spent the rest of the appointment catching each other up on everything going on in our respective lives. Char and

Wes seemed to be slowly making progress. And by progress, I meant that he reached out to double check which flowers he had ordered because his mom was allergic to some variety and was suddenly panicked. Desi wouldn't budge in the slightest when I brought up the weirdness between her and Carlisle. That was a lie, she actually rolled her eyes so far back into her head I thought she would need medical attention and then promptly ended the discussion entirely by shifting to something else.

Time flew by and I found myself wishing I could have more time with them, but when I saw Josh's car pull up outside the salon doors as we were checking out, I realized I was okay with it. The girls and I had a brunch coming up soon, anyways, so we could spend more time together then.

The bell above the door chimed and I watched as Josh took off his sunglasses, eyes immediately finding my own, and a brilliant smile spreading across his face.

"Let me see," he teased. I obliged with a flourish and he oohed and aahed as I did a few silly hand poses to show them off. "Beauitful as always, little minx, even if something is missing."

The girls both choked on laughs behind me as Josh winked over my head at them. He walked over and gave them both hugs and thanked them for spending some time with me before he placed a hand on the small of my back and led me out of the salon. When I looked back at Char and Desi, I saw them both covering their amused faces.

I was sure my own face didn't look any better, except I was of the "fish on land" variety.

"Come on, minxy baby, we have a reservation to get to."

Josh was uncharacteristically quiet as he drove us toward our favorite little sushi spot, *Sue Me Sushi*. The music was turned up, like always, but he wasn't singing along like he normally did.

Instead, he was drumming his fingers on the steering wheel off beat and kept shifting in his seat.

After 15 minutes of this, I finally had enough of just letting him stew next to me. "Josh, are you okay?"

He damn near jumped out of the car from how hard he reacted to my voice and said nervously, "Huh? Yeah, I'm okay! Did you have fun at the salon?"

"I did... Josh, what is going on with you?" I had never seen him like this.

He relaxed slightly, if only because he realized how strung out he seemed to be. "Nothing, sweetheart. I'm just nervous about this meeting tonight. There's a lot riding on this contract and I just want to make sure it goes well. Dad is letting me run point on it completely, so ya know, no pressure or anything."

We finally made it to the restaurant and by the time we were seated in our booth, he seemed significantly more relaxed. The prospect of good food almost always put him in a better mood.

"Is there anything I can do to help with the meeting? I hold a mean poster board and click a button like nobody's business." I hated seeing him stressed like this, so if there was anything I could do to ease it some for him, I would.

"No, sweet girl, just put out good vibes that they will say yes and agree."

Lunch went by even quicker than the nail appointment did and it took me far longer to notice that we were going in the wrong direction on our way home.

"Josh, where are we going?" I couldn't help but look around as we passed by street after street of beautiful houses.

"I didn't want to tell you, but I was able to get an appointment for us today to go on a tour of the house you liked. Do you want to see it?"

"*Double islands?*" Oh my god. He hadn't brought it up since I showed it to him and I just assumed the house was off the market. Actually, when I looked at the listing shortly after New Years, I saw that it *was* off of the market. Maybe the new owners had buyer's remorse?

"The same one. I take it that's a yes?" I nodded like a crazy person. I was going to get whiplash from how aggressive I was being, but I had been *dreaming* about this house. I couldn't believe that he managed to get an appointment. It sold *so fast*.

I had my seatbelt off before we even reached the double garages at the end of the driveway. It was incredible. The pictures truly didn't do it justice.

"Josh, please tell me there's actually a chance we can get this house." If we couldn't and I got to actually walk through that front door only for it to be taken away from me, I would be devastated.

"Oh, something tells me we might have a decent shot at getting it, little minx."

He went around to the passenger seat and opened it for me to help me out of the car. With one hand back to the small of my back and the other in his pocket, he walked us up to the front door. I gave him a quizzical look as he pulled the key to the front door out of his pocket and unlocked it. I also noticed there wasn't a lock box like there would usually be on homes for sale.

He noticed the look I gave him and explained, "Because it's so popular, the owners wanted to keep it quiet and only allow select buyers to view it. I got the key from Greg."

When we walked in, my jaw dropped. I was coming to realize that was the only face I was capable of making anymore. It was so spacious and cozy. I noticed that the owners had similar tastes as we did as I moved from room to room and caught onto the fact that they had some of the same furniture.

He walked me through each room, pointing out all of the different ways we could utilize the space. Our coffee cups in the coffee nook, his own work space in the small office area, a sewing room for me, etc.

It was perfect.

"Come with me, I want to show you the backyard. They didn't post a ton of pictures of it online, but I got a sneak peek from Greg earlier and I think you are going to really love it."

We walked hand in hand through the double French doors, and I was shocked to see a little fairy garden path to follow. The backyard was covered in trees and plants and would have been my kid hearts dream to have adventures in. When we came around a bend buried thick in the trees, it led us to a gazebo. There were twinkle lights strung up everywhere and candles leading the rest of the way.

When we reached the wooden structure, I stopped in the middle and whispered, "Josh, this is beautiful."

I turned to look at him, only to find him down on one knee with a ring box in his hand.

"You really are, minxy baby. The most beautiful woman I have ever known."

Thirty-Two

Joshua

Her hands flew to her mouth, suddenly needing to hide the emotion on her face. She let out a choked sob in shock and I reached my hand out to her in an effort to help keep her steady.

I also just *really* wanted to hold her hand, to touch her in any way she would allow right then.

"I know I am technically a few days early, but I hope you can find it in your heart to forgive me." She laughed some and I felt her small fingers squeeze in encouragement for me to continue.

"Ingrid Morgan, my little minx, I have a really important question to ask you. Just under 90 days ago, you appeared in my life and from that moment forward I have thought of nothing else except the moment directly after this moment right here. Yes, this one is important, but I am far more looking forward to what we become after this. Every single day that you have allowed me to share your home, every night that you have given me the privilege of holding you, I have done nothing but picture our lives together when we are old and grey. When you found this house online, those dreams changed to our kids running through this very back yard, us growing old in our rocking chairs on the front porch, and the holidays we would host. I also thought about all of the food I could cook for you in that kitchen, because minxy baby, you found the best kitchen I have ever seen."

She laughed quietly and I saw the tears swimming in her eyes. She was holding my hand with both of her own now, like the contact alone was the only thing keeping her on her feet.

"So again, I have a very important question, because I can't get to any of those dreams with you if I don't start here first. I asked you once before to take a leap with me, and I need to request that from you just one more time." My voice started to shake, but I couldn't lose steam now.

"So, here it is. Will you do me the honor of taking one more leap and marrying me?"

She hadn't even glanced at the ring I was holding before she dropped to her knees and pulled me into an embrace. My heart stuttered at the rushed, whispered "yes" she was saying over and over again. When she pulled back, I kissed her as easily as it was to breathe air.

"Do you want to see your ring? Desi worked pretty hard on it," I said in mild amusement. I could never not pick on her, but even I was having a difficult time with it that time. I knew our faces matched in splotchy redness and tear stained cheeks.

As much as I hated making her cry, I allowed myself a pass, just this once.

When she finally caught up to what I was saying, she looked down at the ring still safe in the vintage ring box and allowed me to carefully remove it to place it on her ring finger.

"You remembered," she muttered, almost too quiet for me to hear.

I nodded in understanding. "Of course I did. There's still little diamonds, but Desi said you would be okay with those. Please tell me she was right?" I had almost forgotten how nervous I was about the stone choice until just then.

She didn't let me worry for long, though, as she looked back up at me with the most excitement I had ever seen on her face and said, "It's perfect. You're perfect."

I let out a sigh of relief before picking us up off of the gazebo floor.

"Come on, little minx. I have something else for you to see."

"There's more? What about Tokyo?"

It didn't take us long to get back to the back door, and I whispered in her ear right before I opened it. "Sweetheart, *this* was Tokyo."

She looked at me in confusion but when I opened the door, I watched as she quickly understood what I meant.

"She said yes!" I yelled out to all of our loved ones waiting for us inside.

Desi and Char squealed, Wes and Carlisle whooped and shouted out for drinks. My father let out a "That's my boy!" while her own father didn't make a sound. When I looked at him, I saw that he only had eyes for his little girl, a lone tear trailing down his cheek. When he finally glanced my way, he held eye contact and the grin he wore stayed on his lips. He gave me a firm nod before he walked over to hug her tight and ask to see the ring.

"This is the stone from her mothers," he gasped and sharply looked at me. I nodded in confirmation, but said nothing as I let him come to his own opinions. "Joshua, this is perfect. Ellie would have loved this."

"Wait, is this one of the rings you gave Desi at Christmas?" Ingrid asked her father. He just nodded as he couldn't seem to get any more words out. "I'm wearing my mom's ring? Josh-what?"

"It's just part of her ring, little minx. Desi added the stones around it and set it on a different band. I'm sure she can tell you all about it." That seemed to help get her moving further into the house. I walked her over to my record player and picked out an older Paul Anka record.

"Josh, what are you doing? You can't just touch their stuff!"

"Sweetheart, take a closer look around for me." I continued with placing the record onto my player and moved the needle so that it would play *Puppy Love.*

"I noticed they have a lot of the same tastes as us, but..." She trailed off as she started understanding what was happening. "Josh?"

"Welcome home, little minx. You did say that you wanted this one, right? It wasn't some other house?"

"You bought it? When did you do this?" If I could bottle up all of the emotions that she was flickering through, I would. I hoped neither of us ever forgot this day.

"The offer was accepted on New Year's Eve. The inspections came back clear shortly after that. I know I've been really weird lately, but it was just because I was working on all of this," I gestured around us, "and I didn't want to spoil the surprise. All of our friends helped with getting all of our belongings moved in today, well and actual movers. Luckily, I was able to get a jump start on most of my stuff leading up to this, but everything from your old place was today. Please tell me that this is okay?"

"Josh, this... I have no words. You're perfect."

We spent the rest of the night partying with all of our favorite people, celebrating our love with one another.

When I first came up with my crazy plan of getting her to be with me, I couldn't have imagined the way the ninety days would have ended. At no point, did I truly believe that she would end up loving me as much as I loved her. She was this perfect woman that I couldn't imagine my life without and then there was me, just a man obsessed with the ground she walked on.

But she did give me that chance. She took the leap. And no matter how much time goes by, I would never be grateful enough.

So, when I looked over and saw all of the light shining in her eyes, I just knew my own mirrored hers.

Now I just needed to somehow survive what would be our wedding day...

THE END

Thirty-Three

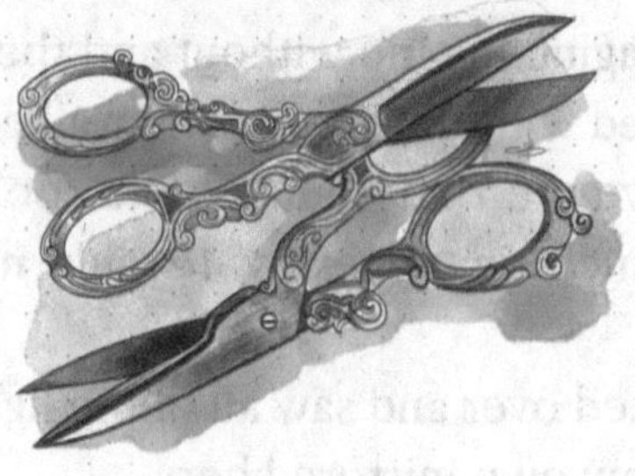

First Epilogue

Ingrid

Seven months later...

"Char, do you have my flowers?"

Holy shit, I was getting married. In a matter of *minutes*, I would be walking down the aisle to get *married*.

"Ingrid, love, they're right behind you in their vase. Do you need me to dry them off?" Desi was already walking toward my wildflower bouquet with lavender sprigs with a small towel to get them ready to go.

Both of the girls wore matching dresses in different shades, a pale green for Char and pale blue for Desi. I suddenly realized we looked like Easter eggs, but it was too late to do anything about that at this point. Luckily, I opted for a destination wedding so at least we didn't look ridiculous in the middle of fall in New York.

Josh and I decided we didn't want to wait until our honeymoon to break in my fancy new passport. Instead, we decided to pay for all of our friends and our dads to come out to a smaller, more intimate wedding in Italy. We found a beautiful venue to hold it that doubled as where we would all be staying.

A knock at the door pulled me away from my thoughts and I looked up just in time to see my father walk into the room we were getting ready.

"You ready, kiddo?"

"As ready as I can be. I feel like I might puke, though, is that normal?"

Char came around and handed me my flowers while Desi made sure my necklace wasn't crooked. My father just stood there smiling at me and doing his best not to laugh.

"It's completely normal, I promise. When your mother and I got married, I actually *did* puke. Twice, if my memory serves me right." He walked over to me and gave me a knowing look that I was convinced only a parent could give. When he found whatever he was looking for, he said, "You're going to be just fine. The boy out there would do anything to make you happy and that is all I have ever wanted for you. I am so proud of you and the woman that you have grown up to be. I know your mom would be, too."

He took my arm and started walking us toward the room's exit. He paused for a moment. "Oh, I almost forgot. You left this next to where you were getting your makeup done earlier." I looked down to see the handkerchief with the blue *"I love you"* stitching. I thanked him softly as I took it from his outstretched hand. After I rubbed my fingertips over the stitching, which he told me last Christmas was done in her handwriting, I folded it gently and placed it into the pocket of my dress.

Yes, my dress had pockets. I made the damn thing, what did you take me for?

My father walked me toward the ceremony doors with the girls trailing behind me. I couldn't choose between them, so they were both my maids of honor. This meant it was up to both of them to make sure that the small train on my dress was fluffed out right, and that the flowy cap sleeves weren't tucked in any spots.

My dress was a blush color with a lace overlay. It had more lavender sprigs detailed within it that took me hours to create and embroider. The bodice molded to me with a simple yet elegant v shape and flowed into an open skirt.

I felt like a princess.

Actually, with the subtle tierra I wore, I really did feel like a princess.

Desi ensured that I wore the earrings and necklace set that she had made me years prior as they somehow matched my engagement ring perfectly.

My mother and I had the same taste in jewelry, it turned out, and knowing that just helped me feel even more like she was with me on my wedding day.

When I heard the string quartet start playing *You & Me* by Dave Matthews Band, I knew it was time for us to get moving. I watched from the side as Char and Desi made their way down the aisle and trusted my dad to know when it would be our turn to begin our walk.

"Just hold onto me, I won't let you fall."

When I used to watch my parents' wedding video, I always loved how my mom needed to hold onto my grandfather for support while she made her way to my dad. Now that it was my turn, I fully understood why she did.

My dad and I turned the corner and *there he was*.

I focused solely on him as I moved. His face went from pure excitement, to genuine awe, to wholesome devastation as a couple of tears started rolling down his cheeks. When he wiped his eyes, he did it quickly, like he didn't want to miss a second of me heading toward him.

He was in his suit with a tie that matched the color of my dress and a sprig of lavender poking out of where a pocket square should have been.

"Slow down, sweetheart. He isn't going anywhere," my father leaned in to whisper. I hadn't even realized I was practically sprinting to get to him.

The moment my hands were clasped in his, the rest of the ceremony went by in a blur. We had already read our written vows to each other the night before as we wanted to keep those private, so we kept to the traditional ones for our actual ceremonies.

After we said "I do" a million times, we finally heard the magic words.

"You may now kiss the bride."

"Minxy love, did I just see you dump that glass of champagne into a potted plant?"

Shit.

"Uhm..."

"Ingrid? Why are you dumping your champagne into a potted plant??" Fuck my life, Josh of course would pick up on what that means immediately. I couldn't have married an idiot?

"Sweetheart, I'm going to need you to say something."

"Oh for crying out loud. Come with me." I dragged him into the outdoor courtyard, my matching shawl covering my arms from the chill and turned to him. "You couldn't have pretended to not see that until after our wedding reception?"

"Ingrid, I haven't been able to pay attention to literally anything other than you since the moment I saw you walk down the aisle. What kind of question is that? You've been trying to talk my ear off all night about how cute Char and Wes were or how weird Carlisle was being with Desi and how we need to set our fathers up with women soon and I haven't been able to do anything but just nod and smile at you because at this point I'm just willing to agree with whatever you say."

Oh boy, he was spiraling.

"Josh, love, take a breath. Breathe." I placed a hand on his arm to try to get him to settle. It worked some, but I could tell his brain was still going a mile a minute and he was doing all he could to catch up with his own thoughts.

"Little minx?"

"Yes, Josh. I'm pregnant. I was waiting to tell you until after everybody left and we started our honeymoon."

"But we only just decided to start trying. You just went off of your birth control a few months ago." He seemed nervous, which was not exactly what I had hoped for.

"I know, I was there. This is still what you want, right?"

He seemed to realize, then, that his reaction was worrying me. He immediately changed from a look of borderline terror to pure concern and then excitement, "Are you kidding me? I'm going to be a dad! How far along are you? Can we tell them yet?"

"I'm twelve weeks, but I want to keep it between us just a little longer. Is that okay? I just want to have something for us for a little bit."

He was nodding his head and smiling, just agreeing to whatever I said, just like what his rambling said he would do a moment ago.

"I'm going to be a dad?"

"Yes, love, you're going to be a dad."

"Husband and dad on the same day, wow, my life just couldn't get any better if I tried." He picked me up into his arms and spun me around, gently, before giving me a kiss that rivaled the one at the altar only a few hours prior.

I truly was the luckiest woman in the world.

Thirty-Four

Second Epilogue

Joshua

Nine months later...

I was wrong before, when I said my life couldn't get any better.

Sure, my wife was squeezing my hand to the point I was sure she would break a finger or three, my skin had definitely thickened after the amount of insults that were thrown my way, and I was pretty sure if I offered her ice chips again the daggers her eyes were throwing would end up becoming lethal.

I was still wrong, because soon our little girl would be entering the world. Soon, I would get to hold baby Ellie in my arms and witness the absolute miracle that was motherhood take over my little minx.

"I might actually kill you for doing this to me." She didn't mean it, she loved me. I was the smartest man to ever man and while I may have seemed like the bane of her existence in that moment, I just knew she would be forgiving me soon.

"I see the head, you're almost there!" the OB called from below the stirrups.

"Hear that? Almost there, minxy love. You're so close now." The death grip she had on my hand only got worse, as did the glare.

"Don't fucking patronize me right now, you don't think I knoOOOW ARGH!"

"Come on, Ingrid! One more push!"

"GET OUT OF ME!"

She was so beautiful. I knew I probably looked like an absolute asshole just smiling at my pained wife, but I couldn't help it. This woman was giving me a child. She was going through all of the pain just so she could become a mother to our daughter when she didn't ever need to put her body through this.

"I'm so proud of you, you are so incredible."

"I hate you."

"No you don't."

I heard the cries of our daughter the same time she did. "You're right, no I don't."

"Congratulations to you both. You have a healthy baby girl."

And then I was cutting the umbilical cord and then she was holding our little girl and suddenly all of her features softened with the pink little baby in her arms.

So yes, I was wrong before. My life could get better. It would continue to get better, because if the look on her face told me anything, it was that we would be doing this again.

"Hey, little minx?"

She looked up, stars still in her eyes that our daughter shared. "Yes, love?"

"Thanks for taking the leap with me."

She hummed and looked back at our daughter, moving the blanket out of her little face. "Thanks for making the waffles."

Acknowledgements

So, how's everybody feeling? Isn't baby Ellie just the absolute CUTEST??? I hope all of the turmoil I put you through with Quinn (AKA Q-Tip, thank you Katie) felt worth it by the end.

Speaking of Quinn... I initially wanted to find a way to redeem her. Ultimately, I decided that creating boundaries, however those may look, was a much more realistic outcome. I knew I didn't want to give other woman drama and I really didn't want to write a third act break up, so I do hope you can forgive me for how much of an absolute *cunt* she was.

Anyways, onto bragging about all of the incredible people in my life!

Nadi, Cassie, Katie, and Ceciley, thank each of you so much for being the best beta readers a girl could ask for. There's no way in hell that I would have even finished this book. Thank you for all of your unhinged comments, your tears, and your encouragement. Proud to call y'all my friends.

For the peeps that have been cheering me on constantly on TikTok, thank you so much. At this point there are far too many of you to name, but please understand how much you all mean to me. I will never understand how me existing on a silly little app and talking to you all on the internet turned into this amazing community of the most supportive people I have ever met. Thank you to the end of the universe and back for all that you do and are.

Kay... You kept me sane during those last rounds of edits. Thank you for letting me yell at you, for calling my ass out, and for helping me understand commas. I'm sure I am still using them wrong, though. Oh well. I tried. Love you so much.

In unison, we all yell, STEEEEEEEEEEVE!!! I still tear up when I look at the art you made me. Thank you for jumping out of your comfort zone to bring my characters to life. I will never NOT shout your name from the roof tops because your talent is immeasurable. Thank you for being my friend and dealing with my bullshit.

Oh hey, I should probably thank my husband right? I mean he got dedication dibs... Fine, fine, I'll do it. Joseph, my love, my life. Thank you for being my biggest cheerleader. This year has been one of the hardest years of my life and without you, I don't think I would have made it. You will never know how much you mean to me. I love you so much.

And last but not least, thank you! Yes, YOU! All of you that have decided to take this leap and read this, thank you for giving me a chance. I never thought I would write fiction. I never thought I would have people that cared at all about what I have to say. I'm just a girl with a laptop, but somehow that was enough for you guys. Thank you for believing in me.

Okay, that's enough sappy shit for now.

Until next time,

B. <3

About the Author

B. Castle is an American author who focuses on providing the world the spice they have been craving. From setting unrealistic expectations for men to making you question your morals, she refuses to stick to just one subgenre of romance. When she's not causing literary chaos, she can typically be found half listening to her husband tell her about Yu-Gi-Oh while she tries to keep her black cat heathen off of her kindle.

Stalk the Author

Website: boundandscorned.wixsite.com/bcastle
Tiktok: @boundandscorned
Instagram: @boundandscorned
Threads: @boundandscorned
Facebook: B. Castle (Author page)